Desire slammed through him

Earlier, Shay had watched her dance as though he'd been under some spell. Seeing her sway and tease, he'd imagined what it would be like to taste her, to feel her body against his. Imagination was nothing compared to the reality, though.

Hot and sweet. Her flavor infused him, left him craving more.

They were in the bar cellar, he struggled to remember, running his hand down her back to where her top ended and warm skin began.

Then he felt her begin to stroke him and he groaned, abandoning his attempts at control in the face of the delicious friction, the tantalizing touch. He pushed her back against the wall of kegs and kissed her hard.

The door at the top of the stairs slammed open. "Mallory, get up here quick. There's a fight," someone yelled down.

They broke apart, breathing hard, eyes wide.

Jeez, what'd gotten into him, acting like this with a practical stranger? At least he knew her name now. And not just any her—she was a woman, a real woman.

A woman who was going to be on his mind, possibly for the rest of his life.

Blaze™

Dear Reader,

I've loved writing the miniseries Under the Covers. I was in the middle of writing *Scoring* when Mallory Carson showed up, a woman with a twist of humor on her lips, shadows in her eyes and a heart of pure gold. Of course, she also had a stubborn streak a mile wide. I got so intrigued that I sent her to Newport, Rhode Island, home of the Gilded Age mansions, and introduced her to pub owner Shay O'Connor. All I had to do then was sit back and watch the fun. They say opposites attract—wait 'til you see what happens when a woman who's as bad as can be takes on a man who's as good as they come. Watch for the Under the Covers finale coming in July 2003, titled *Slippery When Wet*.

Newport is a very special place for me. It's where my husband and I got engaged and has a rich and romantic history, so I loved setting a book there. Be sure to drop me a line at kristinhardy@earthlink.net and tell me what you think. Or drop by my Web site at www.kristinhardy.com for contests, e-mail threads between characters in my books, recipes and updates on my latest book.

Have fun!

Kristin Hardy

Books by Kristin Hardy

HARLEQUIN BLAZE
44—MY SEXIEST MISTAKE
78—SCORING*

*Under the Covers

AS BAD AS CAN BE

Kristin Hardy

HARLEQUIN®

TORONTO • NEW YORK • LONDON
AMSTERDAM • PARIS • SYDNEY • HAMBURG
STOCKHOLM • ATHENS • TOKYO • MILAN • MADRID
PRAGUE • WARSAW • BUDAPEST • AUCKLAND

To my parents, Frank and Ena Louise Lewotsky,
for making me believe in true love,
and for Stephen,
for making it real.

ISBN 0-373-79090-2

AS BAD AS CAN BE

Visit us at www.eHarlequin.com

Printed in U.S.A.

1

"COME ON, DAVE, you want me to have Screaming Orgasms, don't you?" Mallory Carson leaned back in her chair, crossing one long, jean-clad leg over the other as she gave her best smoky glance to the man behind the desk. It was his office, but she owned it now.

Dave gave her a rueful look and smoothed his ginger-colored moustache. "Sweetheart, there's nothing I'd like better than to give you screaming orgasms, but you've already hit your limit for the month." He studied the sheet in his hands. The sheet shook a little as Mallory piled her long dark hair on top of her head with her hands, tightening her skimpy blue sweater over her breasts. "You've only been a customer for four weeks," he protested. "You've only lived here for five. We can't extend your credit line until you've been with us longer. You know the rules."

Mallory had never come across a rule that couldn't be bent, especially when the person in a position to do the bending was a man. "We've been packed to the gills for the last two weeks," she said persuasively. "People drink. How am I supposed to have a bar called Bad Reputation without Screaming Orgasms?" She leveled a look at him. "You're my supplier, Dave. What am I supposed to do?" It was like bluffing in poker, she thought to herself. Stay cool and never act like it matters.

Dave tapped his fingers on the desk. "Business is that good, huh?"

"Business is great," Mallory said smugly, releasing her hair to fall back over her shoulders and trying to ignore the tension in her stomach muscles. "Newport's never seen anything like us before. But it's going to slow down in a hurry if I have to tell customers I can't make their drinks. Am I going to have to go somewhere else?" *Come on, Dave,* she thought, *bite.*

He hesitated, then nodded. "All right," he said decisively. "I'll extend your credit line for two weeks, but I need a good faith deposit of $500 today."

A slow smile bloomed over her face as she let out an imperceptible breath of relief. "No problem," she said lightly. "Cash do you?"

"Cash works for me. While we're making arrangements, let me tell you about the sweet deal I can cut you for your draft beer. We've just picked up the Sam Adams account."

"I'm all for sweet things, Dave," she said lazily. "Tell me what you've got in mind."

IT WAS ONE OF THOSE GORGEOUS Indian summer days when the sky was so blue it hurt the eyes. Mallory drove her little truck along the Rhode Island back road, hauling a load of paper goods back to the bar that had become her life, and pondering Dave's deal. In eight months, when she turned thirty, she fully expected the bar to be ticking along like a cash machine. A far cry from her most recent gig in Lowell, Massachusetts, running a back street sports bar.

She tapped her fingers restlessly on the steering

wheel. Then she reached out to punch a speed dial button on her cell phone, listening to the tone that indicated a phone ringing four states away.

"H'lo." The mumbled greeting sounded half asleep and wholly fogged.

She raised one eyebrow and gave a wicked grin. "This is the Newport Department of Health," she said, pitching her voice higher than her usual husky murmur. "I'm looking for Devlin Carson, partner of record in the Bad Reputation bar. We've had complaints of a salmonella outbreak in your kitchen."

"What?" Dev's brain was obviously still cobwebbed with sleep.

"Salmonella, Mr. Carson," Mallory said testily, enjoying herself. "Your customers have been leaving your establishment weaving and getting sick. We need you to appear to address the complaints."

"But I can't...I live in Baltimore," he said in groggy confusion while she smothered a laugh.

"That's really not our problem, sir. We want answers and we want them now."

"But we don't even serve food. My sister Mallory is the managing partner. She'll..." His voice trailed off. "Mal? That's you, isn't it?"

Mallory gave a delighted giggle. "Rise and shine, sleepyhead." She turned onto Route 38, headed for Newport. "What are you doing still in bed? I don't think I ever remember you sleeping in this late in my entire life."

"Oh, I went out with a couple of the guys last night and tied one on." He groaned. "God, my head."

"Paying the price, are we?"

"This is nothing." His voice was dry. "The price

I pay will be when Melissa comes back from shopping with her sister and lays into me.''

"For going out with your friends? Seems harmless enough to me.''

"She wanted me to take her to dinner last night. I went out with the guys instead. It was Riley's birthday.''

"It's not exactly like you're the world's biggest party animal. People go out once in a while. Tell her it's normal.'' Mallory searched for diplomacy. "I know she's gorgeous and you guys are engaged and all, Dev, but this isn't exactly sounding like premarital bliss. Are you sure she's the one?''

"When things are going right, I can't get enough of her. You just got a bad impression of her when you visited. She can get a little jealous,'' he said, and gave a creaking yawn Mallory could hear over the phone.

"I'm your sister. What's to be jealous of?'' Mallory asked, mystified.

He laughed. "We went out and all the guys were looking at you.''

"She's engaged to you. What does she care who the other guys are looking at?'' Mallory's radar went up.

"Pride? I don't know. I just know she keeps track of stuff like that.''

Mallory shook her head. She couldn't get around it, she didn't trust Melissa as far as she could throw her, however much Dev was hung up on her. "So, what, you go out with your friends and she worries that you're hanging out with loose women?''

"Christ, I got to get some aspirin here,'' Dev muttered. "I'm going cordless.'' The line clicked and turned fuzzy, and she could hear the thuds of his feet as he walked, presumably to find medication. "I don't know, maybe she has a right to be ticked. We're supposed to be getting married in five months. Maybe I should have gone out with her. Anyway, she's always telling me that you've got to give up things to make a relationship work."

That sounded like Melissa, Mallory thought. She'd grown wary of her brother's then-girlfriend the moment she'd found out Melissa was dragging him to couples counseling. Mallory sighed. "Yeah, well, make sure you don't compromise yourself into oblivion."

"I'm just trying to figure out how to do this stuff right. I mean, let's face it, it's not like we learned anything from our parents."

"Sure we did," she said without thinking. "Don't let anyone get too close to you or you'll be sorry."

"You're so tough," he mocked her gently. "Marriage doesn't have to be a bad thing when it's done right."

"Next you'll have me thinking we grew up in different houses. I know you're older than me so maybe you remember their bliss phase, but we both know how ugly it got." She sniffed derisively. "Might as well put a Kick Me Hard sign on your butt."

She heard a snap in the background followed by the sound of water running and guessed he'd found the bottle of pain reliever. "Okay," he said indistinctly, and sighed. "That's better. Anyway, you probably didn't call just to ruin my morning. What's going on?"

"I was just out at the distributor's and Dave offered me a good price on adding Sam Adams draft. Long-term contract. It's still more expensive, but I think it'll pay off in terms of sales. Not everyone who steps in the door wants Bud.''

''You're the manager,'' he pointed out. ''As long as we stay on plan, I'm just a silent investor.''

''Well, the problem is, to go up we need to adjust the terms of our deal with Dave. It'll require a bigger deposit and payment.'' She squinted her eyes. ''Long-term, it'll be fine, but opening costs set me back a bit.''

''I saw the numbers. Looks like business started out slow.''

Mallory nibbled on her lip. ''It'll work out, but I might need a little more working capital next month.''

Dev sighed. ''Mal, I want to help out, but I've got wedding stuff to pay for, too. Are you sure we need to do this? The last set of numbers you e-mailed didn't look too promising.''

''Dev, we've only been open for a month,'' she said reasonably, her hands tightening on the wheel. ''You can't expect to make money on a new bar in the first year. We talked about this going in. We'll be lucky to break even.''

What she didn't say was that if it took walking out into the street and personally hauling clientele inside, she was going to carry a profit back to Dev at the end of the first year. If it weren't for him, she'd still be pouring drinks in small town Massachusetts and saving every penny in the hopes of one day having her own place. He'd taken a chance on her, just like he had all those years ago after their father had died when she'd wound up on his front porch, a teenager with nowhere to go. Now she had something that was hers. She wanted, more than anything she wanted to make a success of Bad Reputation. For Dev.

For herself.

Dev cleared his throat. "Look, Mal, I'm not expecting to make a pile of dough. I'm just wondering if the current financials mean we'd be smarter to hold off on the Sam Adams until business is more steady."

Mallory considered. "I'm estimating an initial 10 percent more outlay, with probably 12 percent more on sales long term. It'd pay for itself in…" She crunched numbers in her head. "I'd say about three months. That's a quick ballpark estimation," she added.

"Did you just work that out in your head? Jeez, remind me again why you're not pulling down big bucks in some corporation somewhere?"

"You have to follow rules in corporations, big brother," she said with a smile.

"And you never were much on those."

"No," she agreed. "Anyway, I'll run some numbers on it and we can talk about it in more detail. And by the way, business is picking up."

"Oh, yeah? Is it something you're doing or is word just getting around?"

"Oh, a little of both." The corners of her mouth tugged up in a smile. "I just sat down and thought about why people go to bars."

"For deep philosophical conversation?"

Mallory laughed. "Nope. Drinks, music and sex," she said matter-of-factly. "We supply the big three and we've got a full house every night. Obviously we've got the alcohol. We're licensed for live music, so I'm going to start auditioning bands for Saturday nights. We can pay for it out of the cover charge."

There was a short silence. "And the sex part?" Dev asked suspiciously.

Mallory grinned. "What did you say? I'm in a dead spot right here."

"Your reception sounds fine to me. You said business is up and you're doing something to make it happen. What?"

"I'm losing you," she lied, smothering a laugh.

"Don't you try to duck me, Mal," Dev insisted, his voice rising. "I know you better than that. What are you up to? You're not going to get us shut down, are you? Mal?"

"I can't understand a word you're saying, Dev. I'm hanging up." Mallory clicked the key to terminate the call and laughed to herself. What she was doing wasn't going to get her shut down.

She didn't think.

"THE USUAL, THEN, DERMOTT?" Shay O'Connor looked at the compact, bright-eyed old man who leaned his elbows on the polished walnut bar, tapping his finger to the lilting strains of a pennywhistle and fiddle playing quietly over the sound system.

"Same as your grandfather served me, young Shay," Dermott returned jauntily, smoothing back what little remained of his white hair. "O'Connor's is still the only place in town that knows how to pull a pint."

Shay tilted a glass under the tap and sent Guinness streaming into it. "The only little piece of Ireland in town, Dermott me lad," he returned in an exaggerated brogue.

"Damned if you can't sound like you came from County Kerry herself," Dermott said, turning to survey the cozy pub. Warm wood glowed on every surface, from the wide-planked floor to the coffered ceiling. Lace curtains softened wide windows that looked out on the gathering twilight. Dark wood panels topped by colored glass divided the combination restaurant and pub into intimate seating areas, forming the backs of long padded benches where regulars relaxed, resting their pints on the trestle tables. Shelves ran around the ceiling holding old books, antique toys and bottles, and a sense of time gone by.

A willowy young redhead with eyes almost too large for her narrow face walked up to set her tray on the bar. "Two Bass, a Guinness, and a Murphy's then, Shay," she said briskly, the brogue of the West Counties running through her words.

"Quick as you please, Fiona."

"Quick as I please would have me taking drinks back to me customers right now," she said with a wink.

Shay eyed Dermott as he let the pint of Guinness settle and started another. "Are all women this impatient in Ireland?"

Dermott nodded vigorously. "Aye, and a good bit worse," he said. "'Tis what drove me here."

"I thought you came to seek your fortune, Dermott," Fiona said with a raised brow.

"That, too," he blustered.

Shay turned his attention to the other drinks. Painted words flowed across the wood above his head: *There are no strangers, only friends that haven't met.* Looking out at the pub, he felt the comfort of tradition filling him like a cup of hot coffee on a cold morning. He put a head on the Guinness and slid it across the bar to Dermott.

A lanky young man with a disordered mop of black hair breezed into the pub. Fiona glanced at him, her eyes lingering just a beat too long. Then she turned, elaborately casual, to check her tray. "Nice to see you've decided to join us, Colin O'Connor, a rock star like yourself," she said, her voice lightly mocking.

Colin gave her an amused glance as he crossed behind the bar. "If I'd known you'd be here, Fiona my love, I'd have left practice early," he said, mocking her accent.

"Sure, and the pope eats steak on Friday," she retorted as she took up her full tray and walked off.

Shay eyed his little brother. "You're late." Both of them shared the dark hair and vivid blue eyes of their Black Irish blood, though Shay kept his medium length for convenience. There, the resemblance ended. Colin had an open face and a boyish grin full of laughter. Shay's deep-set eyes and hollowed cheeks promised something altogether darker and more tempting, like deep, rich caramel compared to white sugar.

Colin tied on an apron. "Sorry. Practice ran over. We were in the groove." He gave a rueful shake of his head. "I tried to hurry but I got pulled over."

The last bits of late summer twilight streamed in through the wide windows. "So anyone know what they're up to at that new bar on Washington Square?" Shay asked casually, his mind wondering about the SOS phone call he'd received from a friend earlier that afternoon.

Dermott waved a hand and scowled. "A lot of ruckus is what they're up to if you ask me. I walked past last night on me way home. Half-naked women dancing on the bar, and all the crowd on the street making a right mess of things." He slurped his Guinness and thumped the glass back down on the bar.

"Should shut them down, they should. 'Tisn't decent."

Colin looked at Shay and raised an eyebrow. "Half-naked women dancing on the bar, eh? Maybe I should go check it out." He made a move to untie his apron.

Fiona set her tray down on the bar. "What's all this about half-naked women?"

"The new bar on Washington Square."

"Oh, the Bad Girls."

"What do you know about it?" Shay asked curiously.

She shrugged as she rattled off her order to Colin, then turned to Shay. "Not much. They only started a few weeks ago."

"Indecent," Dermott muttered again.

"'Tisn't," Fiona countered, leaning an elbow on the bar. "It's just the bartenders doing a bit of dancing when they feel like it, clothes on. There's nothing wrong with it, you know." She flicked a glance at Colin, who was pouring a whiskey. "I thought it looked to be fun."

"Thinking of joining up, Fee?" Colin asked, setting the shot on her tray and grabbing a glass to pull a pint of ale simultaneously.

She gave him an opaque look. "Maybe I should. They seem to get a good bit more appreciation than a lass can get around here."

Colin opened a bottle of Newcastle. "Oh, come on, Fee, you're our fresh-faced young Irish lassie, not a half-naked bad girl."

"Don't be so quick to think you know everything, Colin O'Connor," she said tartly, picking up her tray and walking away.

"That was well handled," Shay said dryly.

"What did I say?" Colin asked, mystified.

Shay shook his head, untying his apron and mentally vowing to stay out of it. "Never mind. Anyway, you can watch the bar. I'm going to head over to see just what they're up to."

"How come you get to do it?" Colin yelped aggrievedly.

"Maybe because I've been here since eleven and you're an hour and a half late?" Shay tossed his apron in a hamper and ducked under the bar walkthrough.

"Yeah? I say it's because you haven't had a date in this decade. You're married to this bar, big brother. It's not exactly healthy."

Shay turned to look at Colin for a long moment. "You have any other observations to make about my personal life?"

"Other than the fact that you don't have one?" At Shay's glower, Colin backed up. "Hey, I know, I know, the family legacy is in your hands and all that stuff. Anyway, abstinence is very hip these days."

"Are you finished?"

Colin grinned. "No, but you wouldn't listen anyway. Go spy on the half-naked women. Be sure to take notes so you can tell me all about it."

Shay snorted and headed toward the door.

"You watch yourself, now, young Shay," Dermott advised. "Those bad girls will tempt a man into all sorts of trouble."

SHAY COULD HEAR THE PULSING music before he drew close to the line of would-be bar patrons standing restlessly near the door, some tapping their feet in time with the monster bass line. If any of them were over twenty-three, he'd have been shocked. He recognized the beefy man sitting at the head of the line. "Hey, Benny."

"Hey, Shay. Why aren't you over pulling pints?" Whoops and cheers spilled out of the open door behind him.

"Thought I'd come on over and see what's new in the neighborhood." And do a favor for a friend. Six years before, Dev Carson had been a contractor doing renovation work on O'Connor's. The two of them had clicked, drawn together by a mutual fondness for sailing and music. Now, Dev was calling for help. Make sure my sister's not getting herself in trouble, he'd asked. Their friendship was too close for Shay to do anything but agree to watchdog the sister he'd never met.

Benny swept a hand toward the bar. "Be my guest."

Shay walked in through the open door and into controlled bedlam.

The music throbbed so loud that the walls seemed to vibrate with it. Colored spotlights swirled above a long bar that ran the length of the room. At least, he figured it was a bar. It was difficult to tell because of the wall of people in front of it. And above their heads he saw the two women.

They danced up and down the bar, whipping their hair, swaying to the music, throwing in the occasional bump and grind. The crowd of mostly young men whistled and hollered at every shift of the shapely hips above them. Blond and redheaded, the two played off each other, now dancing in synch, now doing their own moves, strutting down to the brass poles at either end of the bar to spin around.

The half-naked rumor was definitely an exaggeration. They wore hip-hugging pants and skimpy tops designed to flaunt cleavage and tanned midriffs. Nothing more scandalous than you'd see in the average shopping mall. Shay gave a wry smile. Perhaps Colin was right about him being married to the pub—the duo on the bar were designed to tease, but to him they looked harmless, more like sorority babes on spring break than anything else.

It seemed to work for the rest of the clientele, though, who surged whooping and cheering against the bar, completely involved in every movement. The redhead crouched down on the bar with a bottle of tequila and poured it into the open mouth of a frat boy who was leaning his head back, swallowing furiously while his buddies counted to ten. Then he straightened up, grinning, holding both hands over his head like a prize fighter.

Shay sighed. Even a half hour of this was going to be too much. It was going to be a long night if he had to hang around more than a few minutes.

A CROWDED BAR, that was what she liked to see, Mallory thought as she poured drinks, her hands an efficient blur of motion. Above her, Kayla swung her long blond hair and danced with redheaded Belinda, while Liane and Michelle worked next to her to pass drinks to patrons.

The buzz of the register was its own seductive music, especially after the lean weeks just past. If she could keep the bar full like this on a regular basis, her financial concerns would be only a memory.

"I'm going to take a quick walk around," she said to Michelle and ducked under the walkthrough. Part of running her own place meant being responsible for every aspect of it, knowing what was happening outside as well as in. A good manager knew what was going on in her establishment.

She threaded through the crowd around the bar. A glance outside told her the admission line had doubled from when she'd seen it earlier in the night. "How's the traffic look, Benny?" she asked her doorman in an undertone.

"We're still at about three-quarters capacity," he answered.

She could let them all in, but a line created buzz. Mallory checked her watch. "Keep the line at about six people until eleven, then let everybody in up to capacity."

Benny grinned. "Whatever you say, chief."

EVEN AS ONE OF THE DANCERS stepped down to go back to tending bar, another jumped up to take her place. Bored, Shay stepped away from the crowd at the bar and began to look around. The space was bigger than it looked on first impression. It stretched back beyond the bar area and widened out into a section filled with a couple of scaled down pool tables and some tables and chairs in an area that could double as a bar or a dance floor. Currently it was only lightly populated; everybody wanted to be by the bar, where the action was.

He grabbed a stool by the wall and sat down to watch the chaos. The servers behind the bar were feverishly pouring drinks. Definitely designed to appeal to the frat boy crowd, he decided, surveying the clientele. It made an impact all right, but for how long? This kind of novelty had to wear off sooner or later.

And if it didn't, what kind of a clientele was it likely to draw into the area once word spread?

The song changed and the blond bartender leaped back onto the bar. Shay scanned the crowd and shook his head. *Dev, old buddy, you've gotten yourself into a king-size mess.* Then his gaze fastened on a woman by the door and he froze.

She was, quite simply, stunning. Beautiful in the larger-than-life way of models and movie stars, in a way that seemed to suck in all available light. She wore a snug leather miniskirt and a short, white tank top that clung to her and exposed a tanned midriff where a gold navel ring glinted. A river of thick, dark hair tumbled down her back. Amid all the noise, it was as though for a moment he was in a cone of silence.

And all thoughts of Dev flew out of his head.

2

MALLORY STOOD BY THE DOOR, scanning the crowd for trouble out of habit. Some nights, the torqued up, liquored up patrons could turn on one another like snapping dogs—a possibility that justified having a second bouncer—but tonight they were content to be entranced by the dancer/bartenders, enticed enough to buy them drinks, tantalized enough to make passes that never succeeded. The girls knew the drill: flirt but don't fall. Every guy who walked through the door, of course, assumed that he'd be the exception, and so they were happy to stand in line to get in, just for the chance of seeing and talking to the dancers. It was the source of Bad Reputation's recent success.

Mallory took another glance across the room, and in the sea of faces, one leaped out at her. He wasn't entranced—far from it. If anything, he looked bored. He didn't nod his head to the music, but sat against the wall with a kind of stillness, the dim lighting shadowing his deep-set eyes. The beginnings of a beard darkened his jaw and encircled his mouth. And it was a beautiful mouth, she couldn't help noticing even from this distance.

At the bar, the noise of the crowd spiked as Kayla and Belinda danced together. It was then that she saw it.

A smirk. A head shake. A faintly supercilious look that spread across his face as he took in the scene.

Irritation flashed through her. On its heels came her innate practicality—a bored guy wasn't going to stick around and buy drinks, and he sure wasn't going to recommend the place to friends. Part of the path to success was sending everyone out happy and ready to return. Maybe she needed to do something about him.

Just then, he turned and looked at her. The eye contact shivered through her veins, stopping her dead. Those eyes pulled at her in a way that made everything recede until she was only conscious of them and of the sudden thud of her heartbeat in her ears.

Then someone at the bar rang the cow bell signifying a tequila shot and she snapped out of it. Magic eyes or no, he was just another customer, and the thing to do with customers was jolly them into spending money. She hooked a circular tray from behind the bar and walked toward him.

The closer she drew, the more clearly she could see his face, the black brows and the slashes of the high cheekbones that gave him something of the artist-in-a-garret look, an impression enhanced by the white poet's shirt he wore. His hair appeared disordered, as though he raked his hands through it regularly. But it was his mouth that drew her, full and sculpted with equal parts humor and anticipation hovering around the corners.

She gave her head an impatient shake. This wasn't about getting distracted by a pretty face, it was about turning a wall sitter into a paying customer. It was time to pull out the charm, blast him with sex. He'd be buying drinks before he knew what hit him. Three, she decided, looking at him under her lashes. He'd buy at least three before he walked out.

Mallory stopped and fixed him with a sultry smile. "Welcome to Bad Reputation, sugar. What's your pleasure?"

SHAY BLINKED. SHE WAS HIS pleasure, if he was honest, though he had a pretty good idea that she wouldn't be all that impressed with that response. He'd watched her move across the room in a lithe, flowing walk that managed to be far more provocative than any hip sway might be. Why she'd decided to come his way, he wasn't sure, but he was certainly interested in finding out. Up close, she was everything the glance from afar had promised and more. In another century, she would have had men dueling over that aristocratic beauty, vying to tease a smile from that wide, mobile mouth with its full lower lip.

One slim brow arched as she looked down at him. "I get the impression from the way you were looking that we're not doing a very good job entertaining you."

Shay smiled. "Quite the contrary. I'm very entertained right now. And I'll take a beer when you get a chance. You have Guinness?"

"No Guinness, at least not yet. We've got Bud, Bud Light, Miller, and Heineken."

"Heineken, then," Shay said. She was in a whole different class from the rest of the bartenders in the place. Whoever had hired her had known what they were doing.

She leaned over to collect bottles from the shelf behind him, setting them on the tray. "Is this your first time at Bad Reputation?"

Shay nodded, watching her. She had the kind of face that sucked a man in, that made it impossible to look away, because the minute you did, you started wondering if anyone could really be that beautiful. "Just stopped by to see if what I've heard was true." Not just beauty, he thought. Sex. Something in the curve of her lips and the tilt of those dark eyes suggested abandonment, disregard for rules. Come with me, they said, and I'll show you things you've never even thought of.

"And what had you heard?" The brunette propped her tray on the shelf and looked at him under her lashes.

His mouth curved. "Something about half-naked women dancing on the bar."

"Well, you've got to admit, they're on the bar and they're dancing." She glanced over her shoulder to where the blonde was whipping her hair to the music.

"Like college girls having a wild night."

"You're calling us girls?" She smiled, but her eyes narrowed a trifle in warning.

"Not you, darlin'." He ran his gaze from her long, smooth legs to the sleek curve of hip and waist, to the dark hair tumbling down her back, and up to that fabulous face. "You're a whole different class from girls."

A little buzz went through Mallory at his look, and she gave herself a mental shake. She might be giving the appearance of flirting, but she was supposed to be working a customer. It definitely didn't do to get caught up in it. "And here I thought I'd heard about every line out there."

"I didn't intend it as a line." His teeth gleamed,

and something of the pirate came out in him then. "Did you want it to be?"

For the first time in years, she found herself at a loss for words. To buy time, she picked up her tray. "Let me go get you that beer," she said, and turned for the bar.

It was something worth thinking about, that he'd thrown her off her stride. It wasn't just the good looks—she'd had plenty of handsome men come on to her. There was something about him, some command of his surroundings that made him far more compelling than the usual pretty face. To allow her system time to settle, she stopped for a few more orders on her way in.

When she returned with his beer, he still sat loose and relaxed, observing his surroundings with an almost purposeful air.

"Miss me?" she asked teasingly.

"Every second was an eternity," he said dryly.

Mallory laughed. "I'll bet."

"Hear any good lines on the way back?"

Her pulse jumped. She set a napkin down on the little shelf and placed the beer on top. "I'm at work, sugar. We don't date customers." On the other hand, she was beginning to wonder if it wasn't time to re-evaluate that policy. She stared at his mouth wondering how it tasted.

"So you're allowed to tease but not to close on the deal?" he asked in amusement, putting the mouth of the bottle to his lips to take a drink. "You ought to at least come up with a way to let your customers down easy, encourage them a little so you get a lasting draw."

Mallory raised a brow. "And are you looking for encouragement? That'll be three dollars, by the way."

"I'm probably not your target clientele, but yeah," he said, pulling out his wallet.

It was a challenge. Mallory gave him a smoky look. "So you don't think I can provide a lasting draw?" She was rewarded when his eyes darkened.

"I get the feeling you can pretty much do anything you want to do," he said, holding her gaze until she felt something in her begin to heat and soften. "Then again, I haven't seen you up on the bar."

"Oh, you haven't seen anything like me." The words were a challenge, the tone a promise.

He looked at her. "You're right. I haven't. For you, I'd make an exception and stay. That's why you should polish up your shut-down line. Teasing is a tricky business. Sometimes people expect you to finish what you start." He took another drink.

"I never start anything I'm not prepared to finish," she said coolly.

He tipped his head to one side and eyed her. "Now, that's a thought that'll keep me awake tonight."

"On the other hand, flirting is just flirting. It doesn't mean I'm starting anything."

"That's a pity. And here I was just going to buy another beer," he said.

Her lips twitched. "And it doesn't mean I'm not. You'll just have to buy that beer and see how well I follow policy. Or buy two," she said, remembering her promise to herself.

"And then do I get to see you dance?"

"I don't dance," she said automatically.

He finished his beer and set it down on her tray. "Can't or won't?"

"Don't."

"Really? You don't strike me as the type who would be afraid to be up in front of a crowd."

"I'm not afraid."

"Of course not."

"Get that idea out of your head."

"I don't doubt you," he said agreeably. His smile grew wider.

Was that condescension she saw? "I should take care of the other customers," she said at last. "Are you in for another beer?"

"Sure." He eyed her assessingly. "I figure I'll stick around to see if you get up there. Since you're not scared."

Recklessness snatched at her control, but she held on. Mallory turned without a word and went back behind the bar. Normally the routine of drawing beers and pouring drinks soothed her, but not tonight. She wanted to wipe the smirk off his face. He thought he knew something about her from a five minute conversation? He was dead wrong.

The tinny bang of three guitar notes heralded the start of INXS's "You're One of My Kind" on the jukebox. The monster groove begged her to move, and without thinking about it she found herself up on the bar.

SHAY'S MOUTH WENT DRY. Had he thought that the dancing was harmless? He'd been catastrophically mistaken. Long and lean and the stuff of men's dreams, she moved on the bar with lithe grace, whipping her hips and arms to the beat of the music. Raven hair swung around her shoulders, her eyes fastened on his, hot and dark and full of promise. A teasing smile played over her mouth. At that moment, every man in the room might cheerfully have fought to have her.

But she was looking at him.

The song went on, a tale of teasing and seduction, the moan of a man luring his lover. As she was luring him. Moving to the beat, she mouthed the words and slid one fingertip up her leg, over her hip, across the bare skin of her flat stomach with its gleaming gold ring. Trailing her finger up between her breasts to shouts from the crowd on the floor, she slipped it between her lips, pursing them around it as though she tasted something sweet. Shay felt his body tighten.

The blonde and the redhead climbed back onto the bar to flank her and go through their gyrations, but they were like backup singers behind the lead performer, forgettable and easily dismissed. She and she alone had the crowd surging in a frenzy. She and she alone lured him with the hot promise in her eyes.

Need pumped through him.

MALLORY LEANED HER BACK against the brass pole on the bar and slid down it and back up. She was conscious of him watching every move she made, sitting out in the dimness, utterly still. She was up and dancing because he'd goaded her into it. Now she continued because she knew he was watching. *Slide over here, and give me a moment* she mouthed to him, tracing her hands up her body, then lifting the heavy weight of her hair.

As though their minds were linked, she knew how much she was arousing him. It was as though she were dancing for him alone, swaying for her lover, and her hands were his hands, touching her. The buzz spread through her system.

When the song ended, she found herself stepping down to a roaring ovation. Perhaps she ought to get on the bar more often, she thought. Then again, she'd only enjoyed it so much because of the stranger. She passed out beers and shots quickly, waiting for her system to settle.

"Nice job." The words jolted her system.

She looked up to find him leaning on the hinged panel of the walkthrough at her side, those midnight blue eyes on her. He might have had her up against the wall, mouth and hands on her, for all that she felt his presence. The air between them almost sizzled.

Liane tapped her shoulder and she jumped. "Hey, the keg on line two is out."

Mallory blinked, still looking at the stranger, then registered what she'd heard. "Where's Randy? He's supposed to be working the back."

"He's disappeared. Maybe he's on a break or something."

Mallory cursed as she looked for the bar back who kept them supplied with liquor and fresh glassware. Reliability wasn't his strong suit; strength was. Still, with one tap down, she wasn't going to stand on ceremony. Not that she was thrilled with the idea of wrestling kegs, but there was nothing for it. "Okay, I'll go down and take care of it."

"You're out of your mind!" Liane hollered. "Those kegs weigh a ton."

"You want to tell these guys they can't have their Bud? Send Randy down when he shows up." Mallory flicked another glance at the stranger, then ducked through the door behind her, heading into the back where she could get access to the cold room in the cellar.

She passed the dishwasher filled with glassware and opened the door to the basement. It wasn't that her mystery man was so fabulous, she thought as she snapped on the light and clattered down the stairs. It had simply been too long since she'd had a lover, that was all. Taking a lover had just become too much of a bother. For some reason, no matter how often they said a physical relationship was fine, once she started sleeping with a guy, sex wasn't enough. Suddenly they'd be pushing for more, wanting to get into her head, which was simply not an option. For Mallory, the barriers were high and solid and nonnegotiable. In her world, anything more than sex was impossible. Once you got beyond sex, you ran the risk of giving the other person power over you. The years of watching her father drown his pain in drink were all the proof she needed of that.

The trio of bare bulbs that dangled from the ceiling of the cellar did little to banish the shadows. Along the far wall, the stack of silver kegs gleamed dully. Behind her was the door to the cold room, where the kegs that fed the taps upstairs were kept.

She opened the door to the cold room and stepped inside with an involuntary shiver. Temperatures that were perfect for keeping beer icy cold weren't quite comfortable if you were hanging out in a miniskirt and thong. The sealed door thudded shut behind her. Even though she knew it had an inside release, it always gave her the willies to be stuck inside what was essentially a walk-in refrigerator. The faster she finished this job, the better, she thought, staring at the neat row of kegs with vacuum lines snaking up through the ceiling. At least they kept a couple of spares in the cold room for easy access. Pulling the tap off the old keg with swift efficiency, she rolled the new keg into place and hooked it up.

Shivering, Mallory stepped outside and stared at the wall of kegs. Now for the ugly part—wrestling a new keg into the cold room. It was her strict policy that anyone who changed out a keg always put a new one in. You never knew how much beer you were going to go through in a night, and nothing pissed customers off more than warm beer. She kicked her heels off and cursed as her bare feet hit the chilly floor.

Then a noise behind her had her whirling with a gasp.

3

It was him.

Adrenaline surged through her, mixed with little bolts of desire. "What are you doing here?"

He studied her. "I thought you might need some help. Kegs aren't exactly light."

"Customers aren't allowed in the back. We're not insured for it."

"I'll be careful not to drop the keg on my foot, then," he said, with a grin hovering around the corners of his mouth.

That utterly delectable mouth.

She looked until she realized she was staring, then relented. "Well, if you want to help, I need two kegs from the stacks on the left. I can roll them, I just can't lift them down."

He crossed to the tiers of kegs and brought two of them to the floor with approximately the same amount of effort she'd expend on a bottle of whiskey.

"Guess you keep up your gym membership," she said, struggling not to be impressed.

"Or something," he said, grabbing one of the kegs and carrying it in the cold room.

Mallory took the other, tipping it onto an edge and rolling it along. The grating sound it made was magnified in the close quarters of the refrigerator, then he took it off of her hands.

"Just stack them on that side wall," she directed. "That'll give us enough for the rest of the night, I think."

Back out in the storage room, she looked up at him, studying the hard planes of his face. She was tall for a woman; it wasn't often that a man met, let alone bested her height. "Thanks for coming down to help."

"No problem." The bare overhead lights threw his eyes into shadow, bringing out that pirate look again. It made her heart thud a little. Mallory rubbed her arms and shivered.

The look in his eyes changed. "You've got to be freezing in those clothes," he said, closing his hands around her shoulders.

Heat was all she could register for a moment, heat from his palms flowing into her arms, heat from his body radiating out toward her. It made her exquisitely aware of the fact that a sizable, strong, and extremely attractive specimen of a man was just inches from her. This close to him, she could look her fill. "I wasn't really thinking about the cold," Mallory murmured, staring in fascination at his mouth.

"Well, you could use some warming up now." He ran his hands up and down her arms lightly, chafing the skin into warmth, tantalizing the nerve endings.

"Does that mean you're volunteering?"

His teeth gleamed in a half smile. "I told you, I'm here to help."

"What did you have in mind?"

"There are all sorts of ways to warm you up." He moved in closer to her. "What was it you said about always finishing what you start?" he murmured, sliding his hands down to hers and raising them to kiss her fingers.

She swallowed, her throat suddenly tight. "What kind of a finish are you expecting?"

"It changes by the minute," he said, his voice suddenly sober.

Abruptly she slid her hands up his chest to pull his head down to hers. "I guess we'll just have to see, then, won't we," she whispered, and fastened her lips on his.

Mallory didn't bother with teasing nibbles and pecks. Since his arrival she'd watched his mouth, wondered how it would feel under hers. Now she would discover. She dove into the kiss with abandon, tasting the tang of beer, the spice that was him. His tongue dipped and circled around hers, the silky stroking making her suddenly greedy for more. She made an impatient noise and pushed herself closer to him. The long cords of muscle in his back were sharply defined under the cloth of his shirt. Against her hips, she could feel him growing harder.

Need sliced through her, sharp and intense. She needed his hands on her, his skin against hers. She needed his mouth on her, hot and wet.

"When I first saw you I wondered what this would be like," she murmured.

Desire slammed through him. Earlier, he'd watched her dance as though he'd been under some spell. Seeing her sway and tease, he'd imagined what it would be like to taste her, to feel her body against his. Imagination was nothing compared to the reality, though.

Hot and sweet, her flavor infused him, left him craving more. Her wild, sultry scent seemed to be everywhere. He could feel her breasts, warm and yielding against his chest, and the sensation threatened his control. He wanted to touch her everywhere at once. He wanted her, period, on the floor, against the kegs, anywhere, as long as it was now.

They were in the bar cellar, he struggled to remember, running his hand down her back to where her top ended and warm skin began. He definitely had no business wrapping himself around an employee on the clock and on the premises, but the sound of her soft moan made a mockery of his common sense. Her hands stroked the denim of his black jeans and he felt himself strain against the fabric, against the heat of her touch. Instead of stepping away and getting out, he found himself slipping a hand up under her tank top, sliding his fingers over the soft swell of her breast. With his eyes closed and the noise from the bar only a soft murmur in the background, they could have been anywhere. Then the insistent firmness of her nipples against his palm tore a groan out of him.

Mallory gave a soft laugh of delight. His arousal was an aphrodisiac, and a sudden frenzy of desire tore through her. She wanted to know how he felt inside her, how his body convulsed at orgasm. She wanted to feel him hard in her hand, in her mouth. Hastily she fumbled for his zipper.

Heat raced through him. There was no room for practicality, only for the rush of sensation from her mouth, the warmth of her hand through the denim of his jeans. In the bar overhead, someone began whooping. Then he felt the tug, heard the growl of his zipper. He could tell himself to quit all he wanted to, but his hands still slid over her curves to find the hem of her skirt. "This isn't smart," he said, "we're in public."

"Not at all," she said, running her tongue along his neck. "I know for a fact this is private property."

Shay ran a hand up under her skirt, moving between

her thighs to find her already wet. "What's your boss going to say about you disappearing?" he managed, the slippery evidence of her arousal making his head pound. Feverishly he wondered what it would feel like to be inside her, to have her hot and wet beneath him.

"Don't you worry about the boss," she said breathlessly, her gasps catching as his fingers began to slide against her.

"I don't want you to get in trouble," he said raggedly, as her clever fingers searched him out and wrapped around him.

Mallory laughed deep in her throat. "Trust me, I know she'd approve."

Then he felt her begin to stroke and he groaned, abandoning his attempts at control in the face of the delicious friction, the tantalizing touch. He pushed her back against the wall of kegs and kissed her hard.

The door at the top of the stairs slammed open.

"Mallory, get up here quick. We've got a fight," someone yelled down.

They broke apart, breathing hard, eyes wide.

"The bar. Oh my God." She broke away and lunged past him, rounding the banister and heading up the stairs.

Mallory, Shay thought dazedly, zipping up his pants. They'd called her Mallory. Mallory was Dev's sister's name.

Which meant she was Dev's sister.

Shouts filtered in from the barroom, the sounds of a fracas underway. The noises galvanized him and he ran up the stairs. Whatever was going on, another pair of hands would surely help. He wasn't much for fighting, but in his years of bartending, he'd learned a few nasty tricks that were useful for dealing with rowdies.

As it turned out, his help wasn't necessary. By the time he'd ducked out from behind the bar, the bouncers had grabbed the fighters in painful come-along holds and were leading them out the door. No obvious damage had been done, aside from a stool or two overturned. The rest of the patrons were milling around. The redhead jumped on the bar and began to dance, working to bring the energy of the room back up. Slowly people filtered back toward the bar, but the crowed was smaller than before.

Shay saw Mallory in a corner, talking sympathetically to a weeping girl, and he was abruptly furious at himself. Dammit, he'd been the worst kind of idiot. One minute he'd been sitting in the bar checking it out, trying to figure out what to tell Dev. The next, he'd seen Mallory and she'd driven all thought and responsibility out of his head. He'd gone from chatting her up to groping her in the cellar. He could say he'd gone down to help her, but deep down he knew it was because he wanted to be near her. Needed to be near her. And now he, who always prided himself on being the responsible, trustworthy guy, had wound up almost doing the sister of one of his best friends.

He saw Mallory holding the girl's hands and talking to her soothingly. Just for a moment, the purity of Mallory's profile stopped his heart. He didn't date often. His responsibilities more or less precluded it, but it also wasn't often that a woman captured his interest. All Mallory had had to do was walk into his line of sight. It wasn't just the face, although admittedly, that had gotten his attention first. It was the intelligence and humor that sealed the deal.

And of course the physical stuff.

That was history now, he thought, slipping unobtrusively out the door. He was going to be smart and stay away. If Dev wanted his input, he'd give it, but that was all. He was going to keep a healthy distance from Ms. Mallory Carson. Certain things were unforgivable, and one of them was sleeping with a friend's little sister, he thought, as an image of his own sister, Shana, rose in his mind. Especially when you were supposed to be watching out for her.

Out on the sidewalk, Shay shoved his hands into his pockets and tried to ignore the ache in his belly. Just for a moment there, she'd had him. Despite his best resolutions, he wouldn't have been able to stop for his life. The interruption had saved him from doing something he'd *really* have been sorry for. Walking away had been the easy part. Convincing his body that the time for fun and games was past was a little tougher.

Nice behavior for a local businessman, he thought sourly. Yeah, he'd really make points at the next Chamber of Commerce meeting if word got around that he was entertaining young ladies in backrooms.

Not a young lady, he corrected himself. A woman.

A woman who was going to be on his mind possibly for the rest of his life.

"Night, Mal. See you tomorrow."

"See you," Mallory echoed, locking the door behind the departing Belinda. The lights were on, the harsh illumination giving the bar a very different feel from the intimacy of the night. Scars on the wood and floor showed up, as well as the odd spill. She made a face. Thank heaven for Doug the magical custodian. Cleaning and restocking the bar was one thing—in its own way, it was sort of soothing. However, the idea of facing the men's room after a night of rowdy drinkers was enough to make her shudder.

She went behind the bar and began checking the bottles of liquor, refilling them when necessary, or bringing out spares for the shelf. Truth be told, she was glad of something to do. Even though hours had gone by since her interlude with the stranger, she was still restless, distracted.

He'd walked away on her. They'd been on the verge of having each other right then and there, and he'd walked away like it was nothing. She shook her head like a dog shaking off water. That wasn't the way it went in her world. Men didn't walk away from her. She did the walking away. The one thing she'd learned before she'd even learned to read was that the one who could walk away held the power. The lesson had been branded into her consciousness. She'd learned it and remembered it, and she'd gotten very, very good at it.

The hell of it was, her body still wanted him.

She found herself staring into space and shook her head to clear it. Enough, he was gone, she'd never see him again, and that was that, she thought irritably.

All things considered, she was probably lucky they'd been interrupted. She was a business owner and she had better things to do than make out with strangers in her basement. It wouldn't do much for her authority over her staff if they came across her and some customer, especially since she'd always decreed that customers were hands-off. Sure, there might have been times in the past, but no more. Certainly not with a guy who'd just walk away like she was nothing. Not that she was, of course. She was the one in charge. That was how it went.

The door to the cellar opened and Randy, her behind-the-bar gofer, came out wiping his hands on his jeans. "Okay, I've stocked the cold room. There are a couple of spare kegs for every line."

She nodded and fixed him with a stare before going back to stacking tequila bottles on the shelf in back of the bar. "So where were you tonight just before the fight? One of the kegs ran out and I needed you."

He shuffled his feet and looked down bashfully. "Sorry, I was out back having a cigarette."

"I thought you were going to quit."

He reddened. "One more night. I figure I'll start tomorrow."

It was his problem, she told herself, resisting the urge to lecture him. "Whatever. Just keep it to your breaks, Randy, especially on Saturday night. You know how busy we get."

"I know," he said, grabbing bottles of bourbon to put on the shelf. "I'm sorry. I saw Shay head down to help you, though, and I figured he could handle things and Benny gave me the high sign to come over and help with those idiots who were fighting, and—"

"Whoa, whoa, whoa." She raised one hand. "Stop just a second. Who did you say went down to help?"

"Shay O'Connor."

"Shay O'Connor," she repeated. "I know that name."

"Probably so. He's the guy that runs O'Connor's." He looked at her quizzically. "I thought you knew him."

The burst of anger shocked her. Mallory drew in a breath and worked to stay calm. So the sexy stranger she'd thought was a customer was actually a fellow bar owner from just a few blocks over. She eyed

Randy. "You think he was checking out the competition?"

"I guess," Randy said thoughtfully. "I don't know, he's supposed to be a stand-up guy, but that doesn't mean he has to be dumb. I mean, the place has been drawing a crowd. Makes sense that people are getting curious. You should take it as a compliment."

Take what as a compliment, that he'd conned her? That he'd gotten himself a discreet look around by playing grab ass downstairs? That he'd walked away and left her? "A compliment, yeah. I'll try to remember that." Mallory glanced away. "Look, we're about done here," she said abruptly. "Why don't you head out?"

"Okay." He rounded the bar and walked toward the door, then stopped. "Hey listen, I'm sorry about sneaking a butt. It won't happen again."

"Right. Now go home and get some sleep." She had a much bigger problem than Randy's smoking habit, Mallory reflected as she closed up the back of the bar and got her keys. What was Shay O'Connor doing checking out her bar on the quiet? It would have been one thing if he'd introduced himself. The fact that he hadn't made her wonder just what he was up to.

Someone was playing games, and it wasn't her.

Yet.

4

MALLORY SAT AT HER KITCHEN table, sipping at a mug of coffee with the newspaper spread open in front of her. She'd taken care of her first Sunday priority—the funny papers—over toast. Now she was on to part two—the *New York Times* crossword. Staring at the puzzle, she nibbled on the end of her pen before her eyes brightened and she filled in an answer.

Across the room, the answering machine clicked and began to whirr.

Mallory had long ago decided that just because a phone rang, there was no reason she had to answer it. It hadn't taken her much more time to graduate to turning off the ringer. Now, she was blissfully unaware of a caller on the line until her machine went off, which was fine with her. She had one or two friends who considered her antisocial; she just considered herself efficient.

The machine gave a long beep. "Mal, are you there?" Dev's voice came out of the tiny speaker. "Pick up the phone. I know you're—"

She loped over to grab the receiver. "Hey."

"Why do you make me listen to that stupid message every time?" he asked aggrievedly.

"You know why. It helps me avoid telemarketers."

"Not to mention other people you don't want to talk to."

She permitted herself a smile. "That, too. Anyway, I keep telling you, hit the star key and you don't have to listen to the message."

"Yeah, yeah, yeah. So what are you up to?"

"Working on the crossword. What's a six-letter term for a group of crows?"

"Don't you ever read the news?"

She took a gulp of coffee. "Sure, on weekdays. Sunday's my official day off from world chaos. So how's Melissa?"

Dev blew out a breath. "She's fine now but after you called yesterday, she lit into me as soon as she saw I was hung over. Picked a fight and got nasty." His tone turned grim. "She saw my wallet on the dresser and said I should take her to her favorite stores to make it up to her."

"Oh, real nice," Mallory said sarcastically. "You ask me, big brother, it's time to walk."

"Yeah, well." She could hear a rapid thudding that sounded like he was drumming his fingers. "It ticked me off. As soon as she saw it, she apologized and it was like she was fine. She made breakfast, told me about her day, gave me an ice pack for my head."

Mallory frowned. "And that's supposed to make it all better?" It brought out her protective side. Family took care of its own. "Dev, it's not like getting married is going to change things. You guys are having problems. If things don't work right now, they're not going to later."

He sighed. "I don't know. Sometimes it's great."

"Yeah, well, is there anything I can do? Do you want to take a break and come up for a visit?"

"Thanks, but it's my problem and I'm the one

who's got to deal with it. That wasn't why I called, though."

"Oh, yeah? Then what's up?"

"Well..." He hesitated. "I was thinking about the bar, after we talked yesterday. Sounds like you've got your hands full. It bugs me that I'm not around to help you deal with it."

"I knew what I was getting into," she said lightly. "I don't mind going it alone."

"I've got a better idea."

A shudder of trepidation ghosted over her. "Why do I not like the sound of this?"

"Remember I told you about a friend of mine in Newport who runs a bar?"

"Yes, and remember, I told you I didn't want help."

"Just listen to me. He's got a bar of his own. I've asked him to look in on you, see how things are."

"No!" Mallory said sharply. "This is my show, Dev. I can do this alone. I've been running bars for other people for eight years."

"Relax, he's not going to run things, okay? But he grew up in Newport, his family's had a pub there for about sixty years. I think he's worth listening to."

"I thought you were going to be hands-off and let me run things. Why the sudden change of heart?" she asked, her voice bitter.

"Look," he said gently, "we both know you had a rough start."

"I told you—"

"Yeah, I know you told me. But yesterday it sounded like you had something up your sleeve you didn't want me to know about."

"Dev, I was just teasing you."

"Yeah right." His tone clearly said he wasn't buying it. "Mal, we both know you have this problem with playing by the rules. And that's fine if you can get away with it. But you can't always do that, particularly when it's your ass and my money on the line. I just want Shay to weigh in before you get us both in trouble."

There was a sudden roaring in her ears. "Shay?" she asked carefully.

"Yeah, Shay O'Connor. His family owns a pub called O'Connor's. Maybe you've been there."

Calm, she told herself. The important thing was to keep calm. "I know it. Has your friend by any chance been to Bad Reputation yet?"

"Sure. He stuck his head in last night."

Damn his eyes, she thought, incensed. He'd flirted with her, come on to her, never once letting her know why he was there. The sudden memory of the heat of his mouth swamped her. She thought of the feel of his hard cock in her hand and a thin thread of arousal twisted through her, despite the wrath and mortification. "What the hell does he think he's doing, walking around my place like some kind of mystery shopper," she burst out in fury.

"I *asked* him to," Dev interjected before she could say more. "I just wanted to be sure you weren't doing something we'd both be sorry for." He paused. "Girls dancing on the bar, Mal? Come on, use some judgment."

"Dammit, Dev, it's not like they're stripping or anything," she said hotly. "I didn't plan it. But the important thing is that it's working. The place was packed last night."

"Yeah, Shay said you also had a fight."

"Like that's so unusual in a bar? Sounds like our Mr. O'Connor's done entirely too much talking all together," she said cuttingly. "And did he tell you anything else?" *Like we were five seconds from getting naked?*

"There's more? Mal, this was supposed to be a bar, not a club with dancing girls," he said disgustedly. "Are you telling me you wouldn't be concerned if you were in my shoes?"

His words cooled the anger to hurt. "Don't you trust me, Dev?"

"You know I do." His voice softened. "I think you're the best. But maybe we both bit off a little bit more than you could chew this time."

"I can make this work, I know I can," she said desperately.

"If you were in a leaky boat surrounded by sharks, you'd still be too stubborn to call for help. I want Shay in there. That way I won't have to wonder. I'll know."

She stared at the phone. "Is this an ultimatum?"

"Mal, it's not about ultimatums. Just consider him my stand-in. I can't be around so I'm drafting him to do it for me. He's going to offer advice, that's all. Just go talk to him."

Oh, yes, she thought, she'd talk with him all right. She'd give Shay O'Connor a talking to he'd never forget. "Fine," she said shortly. "If that's the way you want it, fine."

"It's only for a little while, just till things get rolling."

"Right."

"Good." He waited a moment. "And the six-letter term for a group of crows is a murder."

SHAY WIPED THE DARK WOOD of the long bar that ran across the back of O'Connor's and stared moodily out at the crowded pub. Sunday brunch at O'Connor's was a Newport tradition. People came at noon with their newspapers and sat down to an Irish breakfast, or a Sunday lunch of roast beef and potatoes. All morning he'd been pouring Bloody Marys, Irish coffees and ale to go with it.

Keeping his hands busy hadn't kept his mind off of his behavior the night before, though. Memories of his colossal blunder still paraded through his head. He liked to think of himself as intelligent, as respectable, as deliberate.

Instead he'd found himself in the middle of an x-rated clinch in the basement of a local bar with a woman whose name he hadn't even known. A woman who just happened to be the person he was supposed to be there to watch out for.

It hadn't helped that he'd talked with Dev that morning, blindingly conscious of the fact that he'd gone where no man should ever go with a buddy's sister. That thought had almost drowned out the fusillade of questions. "How is the bar? How's the traffic? What is she up to? Is it legal?" Dev's voice, first filled with anxiety, was then overlaid with relief that Shay was looking out for things. "Is she getting herself in trouble? Is she doing a good job?"

Not nearly as good as the job she almost did on me, Dev old boy. Shay threw his bar rag into the sink with sudden violence. If there was a feeling more unpleasant than that of letting down a friend, he didn't know what it was. It was rare that he did anything he was sorry for. Maybe he was living too quietly, though, given that the previous night he'd been ready enough to walk into a bar and try to take one of the employees in the basement. No matter how much said employee might have encouraged it, ultimately, he was the one to blame.

"A bleak face you've got yourself there, Shay," Fiona said, setting her tray on the bar. "You best watch out, or you'll send all these nice, thirsty brunchers running for the door. Two Harp and a Guinness, by the way."

He started the Guinness and put a second glass under the ale tap.

"What's put you under such a black cloud, then?" she asked, taking no notice of the fact that he obviously didn't want to chat.

"What?" He gave her an absent look.

"Why are you in such a mood?" She studied him with a little frown of concern.

"Just galloping regrets." He gave a shrug, setting the first Bass on her tray. "No big deal."

"Ah," she said as though sliding into familiar territory. "Regrets for something you did or for something you didn't do?"

He finished the second ale. "Something I did."

"That's the best sort to have, if you're having them at all. Better to be sorry that you got out and lived than sorry that you never took the chance, if you get my meaning."

"Turning into a philosopher, Fee?" Colin asked as he walked up behind her to tug on her long red braid before ducking under the walkthrough into the bar.

"I believe I was talking with your brother, not your troublesome self," she said tartly.

"I don't believe in regrets," Colin said, ignoring her comment. "There's no point in them. You can learn from mistakes, but it's everything you've done that's made you who you are, so it's sort of pointless to be sorry for any of it.''

"Now who's turning into a philosopher," Fiona jibed, raising a brow at him. "Are you after putting that into a song?"

Colin stared at her a moment and his eyes lit up. "Now there's an idea." He seized a napkin and scratched out a few lines then looked up. "So what's all this talk of regrets? Did you try to get a job as a dancing girl and get turned down?"

Fiona gave him a frosty look. "I'm regretting that I wound up getting a job here with a man who devils me all the time, that's what I'm regretting."

"Oh, you'd miss it if I didn't devil you, Fee," Colin said with a crooked grin.

"Has your brother always had such an imagination, Shay?" Fiona asked, picking up her laden tray and walking away with a toss of her head.

"You shouldn't tease her so much," Shay said, watching her go.

"What?" Colin wrinkled his brow. "It's just joking around. She can handle it."

"She's an employee, Colin."

"Yeah, right. So what's put you in such a good mood? Did you have a few too many at the bar last night and wake up in bed with a looker whose name you couldn't remember?" He tied on his apron. "How was the new bar, anyway? I was thinking I might stop in and check it out."

But Shay didn't answer. He was staring at the door and the woman who'd just walked in.

Or stalked, more accurately, like a tiger after prey.

Fury shouted from every rigid line of her body. Two spots of color burned high on her cheeks.

When he'd been lying in his bed the night before, searching for the sleep that refused to come, he'd told himself that she couldn't be as beautiful as he remembered. He'd told himself that her smooth, flawless skin, her haunting cheekbones were just tricks of the light. Her mouth couldn't have been such a delectable curve of humor and sensuality.

He'd been wrong.

He'd been wrong in so many ways, he thought in irritation, fighting to push down the memory of the heat of her body against him. A face and luscious body alone weren't justification enough to make a man toss aside the habits of a lifetime. He'd had no business putting his hands on her, whether she was Dev's sister or not. The fact that she actually happened to be Dev's sister just made it all the worse. That morning on the phone, he'd done his best to duck out of any further involvement, but Dev wouldn't hear of it.

"She's my sister, man. I'm asking you, just keep an eye on her, keep her from getting too far out on a limb. I'd do it for you," he'd wheedled, and Shay had relented, knowing Dev spoke the truth. Now, as Shay watched Mallory come toward him, he felt that unholy clutch in his gut that had him thinking once, only, and always of sex. But the night before had been the end of it. Dev's sister was off-limits.

Period.

Mallory approached where he stood by the walk-through, her stare unwavering as she came to a stop in front of him.

"Hello," he offered.

Her face was unsmiling, unpainted, and as gorgeous

as he'd ever seen on a living, breathing woman. "I'd say it's time we introduced ourselves. Mallory Carson," she said without extending her hand.

"Shay O'Connor." Something in her cocky, go-to-hell stance needled him even as the whispers of her husky velvet voice shivered through him.

"So I've heard. It would have been nice to know that last night. What I want to know now is, where in the hell you get off coming into my bar and playing secret investigator, so you can carry tales back to my brother?" Her voice rose with each word.

"Now just hang on," he began, rankled.

"Don't tell me to hold on," she said venomously. "I'm just getting started."

"Stop right there." His voice was a commanding hiss that brooked no argument. "You want to talk? Fine, we'll go in the back and talk. This is a business establishment and you are not going to come in here and make a scene."

"You have no idea of the scene I can make when I want to," she said grimly. "And believe me," her voice rose, "right now I really, really want to."

Without thinking, Shay slammed the walkthrough back and tugged her behind the bar, ignoring her startled cry as he pulled her into the back. "Take over here, will you?" he asked Colin, who was watching, bug-eyed.

"Don't you ever go dragging me along like a piece of meat," she hissed, yanking her hand loose from him.

"Then don't you come into my bar shouting and disturbing my customers," he snapped back. "No wonder your brother's worried about you, if you don't have any better sense than that." He led her into a cramped room beyond that served as the pub's office, closing the door and turning to her. "Okay, you've got five minutes to say whatever it is you came here to say."

"Listen, buster, I've got a million reasons to be upset at you right now, so don't even try to shut me down."

Shay dropped into the chair behind his desk and eyed her. "Tough as nails, huh?" So long as she acted like a spoiled teenager, it was easier to imagine that he might be able to go more than a few days without having to have his hands on her.

"Don't push me," Mallory said. "Why the hell didn't you tell me who you were last night?" Fury burned in her eyes.

"I was just there scoping things out. I didn't realize I had to check in at the security desk," he drawled in a voice calculated to annoy her.

"You weren't just dropping in at the new neighborhood bar. You were there to review the place for my brother."

"Who wanted me to take a quiet look and tell him what I thought." He didn't bother masking the edge in his voice. The frustration he'd felt all day finally had an outlet.

"I had a right to know," Mallory said stubbornly, sitting down in a chair by the wall.

"Well I wasn't about to tell you I was checking out the bar. It was Dev's place to tell you, not mine."

"You didn't think it was a courtesy I deserved?"

"Come off it." This time, the impatience sounded thick and ripe in his voice. "It's eleven o'clock at night, the place is packed to the rafters, the last thing I'm going to do is run around looking for the owner.

Anyway, I didn't want to get the happy tour. I wanted to get my arms around the place, see what you were doing with it.''

"Well, you managed to get your arms around a few things quite efficiently.'' Her voice was tart.

"I didn't see you telling me you owned the place.''

"That should make a difference? It's okay for you to sleep with my employees?''

"Who kissed who first?'' he demanded.

If she'd been a cat, she'd have been hissing with her back arched. "You need a razor to help split that hair? You were the one who followed me into the basement and you were just as into it as I was.''

His voice rose to match hers. "Well, one thing I can tell you is it sure as hell won't happen again. It wouldn't have happened last night if I'd known who you were.''

"Or if I'd known who you were. And then you've got the nerve to call my brother this morning and tell him that I'm not handling things properly.'' It rankled even more now that she was looking at him.

"I told him what I saw,'' Dev snapped back. But he hadn't, not really. He hadn't told him about the way she'd looked in the dim lighting, the way she'd danced like an invitation to sin, the way his mind had already had her undressed, twisting hot and urgent against him. He hadn't told him that the image had kept him awake all night.

Mallory stood up and braced her hands on the edge of the desk. "Bad Reputation is mine. Do you understand that?'' She leaned toward him, her eyes dark with intensity. "I don't need some stiff-necked son of Ireland spreading horror stories about it. Thanks to you, Dev's got some crazy idea that I'm going to scandalize the neighbors and get run out of town on a rail.''

''I just told him what I saw.''

She turned around and sat back down, squeezing the arms of the chair. ''I don't know who I'm more angry at, you or Dev.''

''Look, even if he weren't your brother he's your business partner, and he's got a right to information. He's got a right to have input. Besides, where I come from, family looks after family.''

''I don't need looking after,'' she said icily.

''You may need looking over, though.''

''Not by you,'' she retorted.

How could a woman look so outrageously tempting with her jaw jutted out daring him to come after her? ''You keep doing what you're doing and eventually it's going to come back and bite you.''

''I know the regs, O'Connor. Having the bartenders dance on the bar once in a while won't get us shut down.''

''I'm not talking about the authorities. I'm talking about customers.''

She gave him a smug stare. ''Do you want to know my take last night?''

''You don't get it. Newport may be a summer town, but you've also got people who live here year-round.''

''So?''

''So the summer people are here four months max. The rest of the time you're depending on the townies, plus some of the yachty set. You're pitching your place to the summer crowd, but they'll only keep you in business for a few months out of the year. And if you get a rep as a bar that makes the town look cheap, the townies won't come.''

Mallory rolled her eyes. "Please. We've got universities in town. The students will keep me in business."

Dev hadn't told him she was half mule. "Don't you know the first rule of college? Students always have the most money at the beginning of the semester. After a few weeks, you'll notice that fewer and fewer of them will show. Your blue-collar guys, if they want to see women, they'll go to a real strip bar. And you're cutting yourself out of one whole part of your demographic if you set up the bar so that women won't want to come alone." He shook his head. "Not a smart move."

Mallory studied him and her mouth began to curve. "You know, not every woman is turned off by the atmosphere in Bad Reputation. Some of them like it. We've got some regulars—they like the fact that the clientele is mostly men. They like watching the women dance—hell, sometimes they even get up on the bar themselves." She traced a small pattern on the desk with one finger. "I don't think using sex to sell the place is a dumb idea, I think it's brilliant."

Shay shook his head. "You're not getting the big picture. You're setting yourself up for trouble."

Mallory stared at him for a long moment, then she stood up, the corners of her mouth tugged into a dangerous smile. "You think I'm trouble so far, honey? You don't know the half of it."

"Don't try to turn this into some power game. Let's just do the best thing for the bar and for your brother, not something that's bad for both." Shay watched her walk to the door.

"You want to see bad, sweet pea?" She stood with her hand on the doorknob, eyes flashing. "You just watch. I'll show you how bad I can be."

5

THE MIDMORNING SUN SHONE out of a cloud-dotted sky as Mallory ambled along the Newport waterfront, sipping at her coffee. She loved it like this, cool and quiet, empty of crowds. White-topped pilings marched along the edges of docks that were lined with boats bobbing on the blue water. Turn-of-the century buildings ran down some of the older wharfs. Along with the brick sidewalks, still damp from the rain the night before, it took her back to another time.

She settled on a bench that let her look along the cobbled streets and at the old post office, itself a historic landmark. Newport was a town that could be easy to love. Maybe she'd finally found a place she could stay.

She'd grown up first in Newark, then in a dilapidated Philly suburb. After turning sixteen and moving in with Dev, she drifted along from city to city, as they followed his itinerant carpenter lifestyle. Somehow, though, even after she'd grown old enough to strike out on her own, she never settled down. After she'd been in a place for a while she'd get restless, find herself looking for something more.

When the itch hit, she knew it was time to move on. It was part of her nature, maybe, the part that was perpetually dissatisfied with the status quo and craved something different. ''Selfish girl. You're just like your no-good mother," she could hear her aunt Rue's sour voice as though she were sitting next to her. "Always looking for something else." Mallory squeezed her eyes closed.

Maybe the reason she moved so often was to get away from the suffocating sense of negativity that she'd grown up with, their already unstable household torn apart. She remembered the day her world flew apart so clearly: coming home from kindergarten, getting off the bus with Dev, walking into the house, knowing somehow that something was different.

Even at her young age, Mallory already knew better than to expect hugs and cookies when she got home. There'd been times when their mother was at work and times when they'd found her passed out on the couch, a bottle at her side. This time, though, it was different, with an emptiness, a silence that rang in the ears.

And a note on the kitchen table.

Everything after that was a blur—Dev on the phone, the sight of her father's grief and the arrival of her pinch-faced aunt Rue. Then the move, leaving her friends and most of her belongings behind to crowd into Aunt Rue's shabby bungalow in a suburb of Philadelphia. And the refrain that had echoed in her ears right up to the day she'd walked out the door with nothing but the clothes on her back: "You're no good, just like your mother."

Maybe if Aunt Rue hadn't practically raised Mallory's father, she wouldn't have seen the drifter he married as an evil interloper. Maybe if Mallory had gotten her father's light hair and blue eyes instead of her mother's dramatic Mediterranean coloring, Aunt Rue wouldn't have treated her as a stand-in for all that she hated. Maybe if once, just once, her father had stuck up for her, Mallory would have stood a chance.

"Enough," Mallory muttered, opening her eyes to stare hard at the water. It was the past, and done. Dev had escaped as soon as he could, unable to continue watching their father's slide into a silent alcoholism. When a freak dockside crane collapse had killed her father, Mallory figured she had two choices—stick around and see how bad it could get or find Dev and hope to God he'd take her in.

The fact that he had, without hesitation, made her eternally grateful to him. Almost grateful enough to get over wanting to strangle him for his great idea about Shay O'Connor.

Shay O'Connor...a frown settled over her features as she watched a boat come into the dock. How was she going to get him out of Bad Reputation? It was hers, she thought. She was the owner, Dev the silent partner, that had been the arrangement. Only Dev'd never been able to break himself of being her big brother. God knew he'd gotten her out of trouble enough times when they were kids that maybe she shouldn't blame him for thinking she needed to be bailed out of this one.

The thing was, though, she didn't need to be bailed out. She knew exactly what she was doing and while her long-term plan maybe didn't call for dancing girls on the bar, the short-term sure did. So now she was saddled with a watchdog who seemed dead set on complicating everything she tried to do.

How to get out of it, that was the question. Much though she itched to tell Dev to take a hike, she simply couldn't do it. It was out of the question: she owed him too much. She could accomplish the same thing by getting Shay to quit, or at least getting him under her sway. There had to be a way to distract Shay from his purpose. No one was perfect, not even him.

She took a sip of her coffee and stared along the waterfront. It was too bad that she had to be at odds with O'Connor when he was so purely and simply gorgeous. Even the previous day when she'd been spitting mad at him, some part of her brain had still registered the magnetism of that carelessly handsome face, the fascination of those strong, long-fingered hands. It made it hard to hate him properly when her libido was busily imagining just what it would be like to have those hands all over her, to be able to taste that delectable mouth of his at her leisure, to be able to…

She sighed and leaned an arm on the back of the bench as she pondered. Then a slow smile began to spread over her face. Perhaps there was a way out of this after all, a way she could have her cake and eat it, too. Maybe the thing to do was seduce him. Seduce him, she thought with an unholy flutter in her gut. If she did it right, she'd have him so focused on her that the last thing he'd think about would be the bar. He was such a straight-up guy that if he slept with her, he might even give up on the whole watch dog thing entirely. Either way, she couldn't lose.

But the best part was that for a while, at least, she could have her fill of him. Sex without complications, for once in her life. After all, he could hardly give her a tumble and explain to Dev they'd been sleeping together. No, they could have a purely physical fling that would satisfy both of them. After what she'd felt and tasted and touched that night in the bar, she could say that with full confidence.

Mallory got up and began to walk in high good humor. She'd head back to the office, finish some of the paperwork and go find— She froze, staring down the street at none other than Shay O'Connor, stepping out of a shop on Thames Street and walking away from her. Oh, it was too perfect, she thought, dragging her hands through her hair to tousle it and pinching color into her cheeks. Yep, sometimes things were just meant to be.

SHAY TURNED AT THE SOUND of his name to see Mallory Carson walking toward him, leggy and quick in jeans and a jacket, her loose hair flying in the breeze. She was off limits, he reminded himself, but that didn't mean he had to like it.

He eyed her. After the way she'd stomped out of his office the previous day, he did an automatic check for weapons before relaxing.

"I thought that was you," she said as she walked up. "Doing some shopping?" There was an energy humming around her that made him uneasy. Something in her manner suggested that he was exactly what she was looking for, and he was pretty sure that wasn't the case.

"An errand or two. How about you?"

"I just like walking along the waterfront in the morning. Clears my head." She tossed her paper coffee cup in a nearby trash can. "I also wanted to look into some of the restaurants along here. We've got a full kitchen and we're licensed to serve food. I'm trying to figure out how deep I want to get into it." She looked at him speculatively. "I'd be curious what you think."

The words sounded a little stilted. Given the tenor

of their previous conversation, it was hard to believe that she'd had such a dramatic change of heart. He gave her a skeptical look. "What happened to the woman who wanted to strangle me yesterday?"

She shrugged and glanced away. "Maybe I'm resigned to my fate."

Somehow she didn't strike him as the type to see reason that quickly. Based on what he'd seen, he was pretty sure she had a stubborn streak a mile wide and two miles deep. "You suddenly saw the light?"

"Don't look so suspicious. Cut me some slack."

"Hey, I'm all for epiphanies." And he wasn't born yesterday. Something was up, he could smell it.

Mallory stopped in front of the doorway of a café that doubled as a tourist magnet.

"The Brickworks?" He raised an eyebrow.

"Look, let me buy you lunch and make it up to you. We can talk about my plans. Unless you have to be somewhere."

He told himself it was curiosity. It wasn't that he couldn't make himself walk away from that fabulous face while her scent rose around him. He shrugged. "I've got time."

"Great."

Inside, they nabbed one of the few remaining tables. Even on weekdays, the Brickworks was a powerful draw.

Mallory spread her napkin over her knees. "Good thing I'm not starting a restaurant. I'd hate to go up against some place as entrenched as this."

"Newport's a tough market, not least because it changes throughout the year. It's easy to stumble." The way he'd stumbled for her.

"Hopefully I won't do too much of that." She

opened the menu and scanned it. "I know food can be a hassle of its own, but I figure it's a good way of keeping clientele from going somewhere else. We get 'em to spend more money and with food in their stomachs, they'll be able to drink longer."

"What are you going to serve?"

"I haven't thought it through all that much at this point. Bar food, I suppose, with three or four obvious crowd pleasers. We don't want to put a lot of resources into it when we're just getting started."

"You definitely want to go into it cautiously, the way you are. I'm surprised. I'd have pegged you for the...ambitious type," he said. "No offense."

Mallory slanted him a look. "None taken. Now, see, I already had you down as the cautious type. Doesn't it ever get frustrating, though?"

"What do you mean?" He glanced up at her.

"Being cautious all the time. Don't you ever get the urge to say the hell with it and just go for what you want?"

For a brief, inescapable moment, his imagination painted exactly what he wanted—her, hot and steamy and naked against him.

The waitress interrupted them to take their orders and Shay jolted. He watched the mischievous look flicker over Mallory's face as she ordered an array of bar food.

"Onion rings, potato skins, jalapeño poppers and French fries? Are you paid up on your medical insurance?" he asked dryly.

Fun glimmered in her eyes. "I'm doing research. Who knows, I might wind up stealing their chef."

"Their chef's name is Andre and he's the son-in-law of the owner. He's not going anywhere."

"How'd you know that?"

"I tried to steal him two years ago," he said blandly.

The waitress set down their drinks and Mallory stripped the paper off her straw. "So we were talking about going for it, I believe. And do you ever?"

"Rarely. It's generally a luxury I can't afford."

Mallory gave him a sidelong glance. "How can such a gorgeous, sexy man be such a hopeless stuffed shirt?" she asked aloud, pouring a packet of sugar into her tea. Flicking a glance at him, she licked the stray crystals off her fingertip, sucking on it for a moment, her eyes on his.

Shay shifted in his chair, suddenly aware that his thoughts had nothing to do with the question of Mallory's bar. "Don't be so sure you have me pegged. I might surprise you."

"Like you surprised me by coming on to me at the bar when you were working for Dev? Relax," she waved him down, "I've forgotten it. More or less." She gave him an enigmatic smile, then looked around the restaurant. "So is the Brickworks competition for you? It goes after the family crowd like O'Connor's does."

He moved his shoulders and tried not to think of the way she'd looked licking her fingers like a smug cat going after cream. "O'Connor's is more about local people than visitors."

"Did you plan it that way?" Now her face just showed curiosity, and he relaxed a little.

"My great-grandfather did. He started it as a place for the Irish workers to feel at home. There weren't so many places like that back then."

Mallory's eyes widened a bit in surprise. "O'Connor's has been around since your great-grandfather's time?"

Shay watched her, a faint smile on his face. "Look around next time you come in. The building's been there since the turn of the century. We've kept it up."

"I'll say. You really love it, don't you?"

"It's part of our history, part of who we are as a family." But the other part of it, what he only rarely admitted to himself, was that lately he'd been feeling suffocated. He'd lived for O'Connor's since he'd turned sixteen. Lately he'd been itching for something more.

"So your great-grandfather started it, then your grandfather took over, then your father, then you?"

"Not quite. My father was never a part of the chain."

"Ah." Her eyes brightened. "A black sheep? I have a soft spot for black sheep."

"Sort of. He decided he wanted to be a lawyer instead of pull pints of stout. I took over from my grandfather when I was twenty. I'd been working for him for about four years by then, so I knew the business."

"You've been running a seven-day-a-week business since you were twenty?"

"My grandfather consulted at first, but he was in his seventies by then, so it was definitely time."

"No wonder you're so sedate," she murmured, propping her chin on one hand. "Did you ever have a chance to get wild at all?"

"Some." When he'd been able to get away, which hadn't been all that often. "But we had a tradition to keep going and I was entrusted with it. That's part of what Newport is about is history and tradition. You have to respect that."

"I do respect that. I just think there's room for the new as well as the old."

"I agree. It's just the type of new that we differ on."

She studied him. "So are you going to grow old and die running the family business before passing it on?"

"I don't know that that's my dream."

"Oh really?" She leaned forward. "And just what are your hopes and dreams, Shay?"

"Music," Shay said, apparently deciding to take her question seriously. "Running a club for local music. We could also get some good alternative bands between gigs in Boston and New York."

She could see him doing it, she realized suddenly, and her picture of him changed. "But what about O'Connor's?"

"What about it? We've been hosting a live music night on Sundays for a couple of years now, so I'm used to booking bands. I've been looking around at local spaces, getting estimates on rebuilding. I tried to get the space you leased for Bad Reputation, only you beat me to it," he finished with a wicked grin.

She remembered bullying the real estate agent as he tried to stall her for some unfathomable reason. Now she knew why. "There are other places."

"Sure. Location is the only glitch. It has to be close enough to O'Connor's that I could bounce between the two, at least at first."

"When's all this going to happen?"

He sighed and tried not to be impatient. "When the time's right. Right now I'm just doing the background work."

"What's your family going to say? Or do they know about your idea?"

"Not yet."

Mallory studied him and a mischievous light flickered in her eyes. "You know, if you've never had a chance to say what the hell growing up, maybe now's the time. Maybe this is your chance for big bad Shay to come out in the open." She leaned closer to him and suddenly her scent was all around. "Or maybe I can be your bad influence."

Just then, the waitress walked up to set their plates on the table. Shay watched in bemusement as Mallory slathered the various plates with ketchup, then salt indiscriminately. "Purely for purposes of menu research, you said?" he asked, watching Mallory bite into an onion ring and close her eyes in bliss, wondering if she looked the same way when she was making love.

"God that's good. Now what were you saying?" She speared a fry and flicked a glance at him.

BACK OUT ON THE STREET, they drifted along together, each reluctant, perhaps, to split up. She'd enjoyed the time far more than she'd expected to, Mallory realized. Granted, she'd been attracted to him, but she hadn't expected to actually like him. It made her a little uneasy. He wasn't going to get over with her, though. He was the enemy and she needed to stick with her plan. She knew he was attracted to her, she'd seen it in his eyes. All that remained was to close on the deal.

"Newport's a mix all right," she said, gesturing at the line of storefronts on the cobbled street where T-shirt and souvenir shops vied for attention with upscale clothing and housewares stores. It was, she mused, an interesting juxtaposition.

"Something for everybody, I suppose."

"Well see, that's all I'm trying to do with Bad Reputation, provide something for everybody. You give people family and tradition. We give people a place to get wild and sexy. You don't have anything against sex, do you?"

Amusement quirked the corner of his mouth. "Not in principle."

"Don't tell me you abstain? Now that truly would be a tragedy." She caught sight of the next store in the row and her eyes lit up. "This reminds me," she improvised, "I've been thinking about giving the Bad Girls a uniform." And she pulled him through the door before he realized where he was.

The store looked like the inside of a Victorian lady's boudoir, all voluptuous femininity underlaid with sex. Lace teddies hung next to filmy negligees, slippery satin bras begged for the touch of a male hand.

"Don't even think about putting your bartenders in lingerie."

Mallory laughed at him. "Don't worry, I wouldn't. I was just yanking your chain. I need to look at a couple of things while we're here, though."

"Shopping," Shay muttered. "What is it with women and shopping?"

"Buying lingerie's more of a gift for the man than the woman," she pointed out, picking up a transparent babydoll and draping it across herself. She caught the flare of heat in his eyes before he turned away scowling, his hands jammed in his pockets.

"I thought we were going to go look at the books for your bar."

"We are. I just need to get something and we're right here. It'll only take a minute." She picked up a backless wine-colored lace bodysuit that was more open space than fabric. "So, Shay, are you a lace man or a silk man?"

"Try on your stuff and let's get out of here."

The clerk approached. "Are you looking for anything special?"

Mallory hooked a long, black chiffon negligee that was slit up to the hip and cut down to the waist. "I think I'm all set, thanks. Where can I try this on?" The saleswoman led her toward the dressing rooms at the back of the store, then turned to take care of a pair of women who'd just stepped in the door.

"I'll just wait for you outside," Shay said.

"Oh come on, stick around. The salesclerk's busy. What if I need a different size? This is going to take a lot more time if I have to get dressed just to go out and get a little skimpy bit of nothing like this."

Black lace, Shay thought, following her to the little foyer tucked away in the back with the dressing rooms. Why did she have to choose black lace? If she'd stuck with the plain white cotton undershirts at the front of the store, he would have been fine. Instead she was waving around little filmy scraps of midnight designed to make a man's mind into mush.

He listened to the clank of hangers behind the floor to ceiling door and couldn't help imagining her getting undressed, stripping off each garment until she was naked and pulling on one of those skimpy outfits. Lingerie designers understood that the female body was a hundred times more alluring with a few scraps covering it, begging to be pulled off. Something about the tiniest bit of coverage made a man immensely aware of the warm skin beneath.

"Shay. Can you come here a minute?" Mallory's

voice called him softly from the dressing room. He stepped over to the door cautiously. "Can you please get this for me in the next smaller size? It's on the rack by the cash register." She opened it just a crack and slid the lace bodysuit out. He caught a glimpse of her in a firecracker-red bra and underwear and nothing else.

And all the blood in his body went south.

He concentrated, running through inventory of the beer at O'Connor's, counting the number of weeks until the Christmas season started, thinking about the World Series, thinking about anything other than how she'd looked. When he was sure he wouldn't embarrass himself, he went out of the little alcove and into the store. The confusion of lace and straps and silk only kept his mind running in the same circle, like a hamster on a wheel: the way she'd looked, sexy, reckless and sinful.

He found the suit she wanted and brought it back to the dressing area, pleased that his system was calm. He knocked on the door. Mallory opened it and pulled him inside before he registered what she was doing.

"What the hell—" he began, but she put her fingers on his lips.

"Shh, they're coming. You don't want them to know you're in here, do you?" She pressed him down on a bench in the corner.

Indeed, he could hear the salesclerk approaching with her other customers, unlocking the changing rooms to let them in. That was the last thing he needed, to be found in the dressing room with Mallory.

The clerk knocked on Mallory's door. "Everything all right in there? You need anything?"

"I'm just fine, thanks," Mallory called, piling her

hair up on top of her head with her hands. She wore a transparent black babydoll over a bra and panties, the filmy material floating over the sleek curves of her waist. Shay's heartbeat thundered in his ears.

"What the hell are you playing at?" he growled.

Mallory gave him a smoldering stare full of promise. "I have a few more things to try on," she said, her voice barely above a whisper. "It's more interesting to have company."

"I don't want to see you try things on."

"Oh, don't you?" She sank down on his lap, straddling him. "I thought you seemed pretty interested the other night. Just because we're working together doesn't mean we can't have a little fun." She nuzzled his ear and his hands came up around her waist of their own volition.

He forced himself to drop them, forced himself to ignore the husky throb of her soft voice. "Your brother is my friend and I am not going to do this." Oh, but he wanted to. God help him, he thought as he felt her lips nibble on his jaw, he wanted to.

The noises of the women in the dressing rooms next door came through the walls faintly. Each room was isolated entirely from the next, the walls decorated with gleaming light fixtures and creamy striped wallpaper, and topped with ornate crown moldings. He looked across the tiny room and saw Mallory reflected in the mirror on the back of the door, sleek and curvy and enticing.

"Relax, Shay," she whispered. "What, you think no one's ever done this before? I'm sure people have had sex in these dressing rooms far more often than you'd think." She nipped at his lips, sending little shocks through his system. "And I certainly think they've done this." And then her mouth was on his.

He tried, oh he tried not to dive into the kiss. There were people nearby, he needed to keep his wits about him. But the silky feel of her lips, the soft stroke of her tongue against his pulled him into the dark quicksand of desire. Her hair slid against his face, smelling of some subtle and utterly female scent. He reached out, intending to put his hands on her waist and stand her up, but instead found himself sliding them around her as she flowed up against him. Sweet and spicy, her flavor tempted him.

A knock on the door made him jump. "Are you doing all right in there?" the salesclerk asked briskly.

Mallory raised her head. "Just fine, thanks."

When she moved toward him again, Shay put his hands on her shoulders. "No." The door to the dressing room next to them thumped open and he heard a murmur of voices as the person inside left.

"Why not? You know you want me, Shay."

The hell of it was, he did, so much that it was like broken glass in his belly. "What I want and what I'll take are two different things," he told her unsteadily. "We are not going to do this." He stood up and walked to the door, listening for a moment before slipping out.

HE WAS WAITING FOR HER at the curb outside of the store. Mallory couldn't resist poking at him a little. "Couldn't handle all that lingerie hanging around?" she asked dryly.

He was furious, that much was clear. "No more little stunts like that, understand? I've got a business reputation to maintain in this town and I won't see it compromised—''

"—by my irresponsible behavior?" Mallory finished for him in lazy amusement.

He shot her a look. "If Bad Reputation didn't mean something to you, you wouldn't give a damn about me getting involved and you wouldn't be trying so hard to scare me off. Your act doesn't hang together, and frankly, it's tedious." He started down the street without a backward look.

It took her a minute to recover from his shot and catch up with him. "Lectures, Shay?" Lectures had always given her the urge to misbehave. "Now who's putting on an act? Stop taking yourself so seriously and be flattered that you're so irresistible." She trailed a fingertip down his cheek and grinned when he swatted it away.

"This isn't a game," he growled.

"Sure it is. And you're the prize."

She laughed at his expression. "Look, Shay, it's as simple as this. I don't like you breathing down my neck about the bar. You don't like me coming on to you. So as the old saying goes, I guess we've both got to deal with a few things we don't like."

"You're making it a whole lot worse than it is."

"I could say the same to you." She stopped and faced him four square. "Leave me to run the bar myself and I'll keep my distance. As long as you're coming around, though, I'm going to do my best to seduce you." She leaned in toward him until her lips grazed his ear. "And let me tell you, Shay, my best is pretty damned good."

6

THERE WAS SOMETHING ABOUT black ink that did a body's heart good, Mallory thought as she entered the previous night's figures in her accounting program, a can of Pepsi at her elbow. According to her spread sheet, Bad Reputation was not only pulling in a profit on the weekends, it was meeting costs during the week. "Up, up, up it goes, where it stops, nobody knows," she muttered, humming tunelessly. She was on a solid enough footing to stock the kitchen and pay the cook she'd hired to work weekends. When Mr. Busybody O'Connor got around to reviewing the books, he was going to have a surprise coming to him. She smiled, remembering how he had stomped off the previous day.

The phone rang and Mallory picked it up absently, saving her changes in the computer. "Bad Reputation."

"It's Shay."

"Why, Mr. O'Connor," she exclaimed, her voice ripe with false pleasure. "What a coincidence you should call. I was just thinking about you."

"It's too early in the day for voodoo, Mallory."

"Now that's an idea with potential," she said consideringly. "Just think, if you find your physical urges overcoming your principles, you'll never know if it's your own hormones or if it's black magic."

"Great. Something to look forward to."

"You play hard to get, Shay, but I know better," she said teasingly.

"Well, here's something else you should know. I just got back from the Chamber of Commerce meeting."

"If I'd known you were that hard up for something to do, I'd have come over right away to distract you. You should have called me." She took a swig of Pepsi.

"You're a regular laugh riot."

Mallory laughed. "So how was the meeting? I suppose if I were smart, I'd join," she added reflectively.

"Under normal circumstances, I'd agree. In this case…well, will it surprise you at all to know that Bad Reputation came up in conversation before the meeting?"

It figured, she thought. "I'm pleased to hear we're making a name for ourselves."

"It was in the context of parking issues, making Newport look bad, bringing in undesirables, etc. There was a movement in some quarters to have the city check into whether bartenders dancing on the bar is legal."

Mallory's voice was smug. "I'm way ahead of them. Do you really think I'd have something going on in my bar that was against code?"

"Good to know you've done your homework."

"God lies in the details, Shay, and I look after mine." Though she tried to keep her voice light, a bit of annoyance slipped it. "So basically what you're telling me is that the local business mafia met and had nothing more productive to do than sit around and trash nontraditional businesses. And did you join them?''

"Of course not," he said impatiently. "They were crying wolf about it and I told them so."

It surprised her. "You came down on my side against the forces of purity?"

"Mallory, this isn't a joke. You need to pay attention to this." His voice was serious. "You can't ignore these folks. When people like Julius Sweeney and Mary McGuffin talk, the mayor listens. So do the police and the Department of Health. You have to understand how things work."

"I do," she said coolly. "Business rackets are nothing new. It means that when word gets out we're starting to have live music, I can expect to have my permits questioned."

"You already have a live music permit?"

"I applied for everything at the beginning. I figured it was a good way to avoid hassles."

"Smart."

"I have my moments."

"So I'm seeing. Is there any point in suggesting that you don't want to book some death metal band that's going to get everyone all riled up?"

She nibbled on her lower lip. "Well, you do know the price of weighing in with your opinion, Shay."

"I'm willing to chance it." Humor ghosted his voice.

"Well, if you're dead set on testing yourself, I'm auditioning a band next Monday night."

"They don't do daytime auditions?"

She grinned at the question. So he'd been hoping for something nice and safe, had he? "They've got day jobs. Besides, I want to see them in action. Bad

Reputation needs a band that's going to drag people onto the dance floor.''

"Have you got someone you can trust to run the place?"

She leaned back in her desk chair and scowled at his question. "It's a Monday night, for crying out loud. It's not like we're a sports bar. I've worked every night since we opened six weeks ago. I'm overdue for an evening off." Her voice turned silky. "But I can certainly understand if you can't pull yourself away from O'Connor's. I'll be sure to give you a full report," she added smoothly.

"Don't bother. I'll go with you."

Too much to hope she could have gotten out of it, she thought. "I admire a man who's not afraid of a challenge."

"I look at it as less a challenge than an education. Speaking of which, do you have plans for tomorrow during the day?"

Mallory glanced at the calendar on the wall. "Nothing scheduled, why?"

"There's something I want to show you."

Her mouth curved. "Are you asking me out on a date, Shay?"

"Hardly. Consider it more of a field trip. I'll pick you up in front of Bad Reputation at ten."

MALLORY LEANED ON THE FRONT wall of Bad Reputation, looking out over the tiny park that constituted Washington Square. Traffic zipped around the odd-shaped quadrangle, headed off in any one of a number of directions. Clearly Newport had had some city planning early on, but it hadn't extended to anything remotely resembling a grid. One of the charms, and occasional annoyances, of living in a town that had its heyday more than a hundred years before was the tangle of streets that intersected at obscure angles, frequently dotted with parks to further tangle the intersections. The same characteristics that made driving hellish made for charming walks, though, and Mallory figured the good balanced out the bad.

She wondered if she'd ever say the same about Shay. She frowned at the low, black wrought-iron fence that encircled the park, wondering just what he was up to. Be patient, he'd said. That particular quality was not her strong suit, but wondering about it all night while she was pouring drinks had made her none the wiser. In all honesty, she hadn't a clue what to expect. It gave her a little buzz of anticipation.

A gold-colored Volvo station wagon turned the corner and she stepped forward in anticipation. It was so Shay—practical, safety conscious, conservative. She swept her hair out of her eyes, but only watched in surprise as the Volvo swept by.

Perhaps she should reevaluate. He didn't seem the type to put a lot of money into a car. He'd probably drive some midprice sedan, or maybe a light truck. Yep, that was it, she thought, as a turquoise truck swirled around the square with the traffic and slowed as it approached. Practical, but the color was the tiniest bit edgy. That was Shay living wild, she figured. She stood hipshot and gave an inviting smile.

The driver, who wasn't Shay, tapped out his appreciation on his horn as he zipped by. Disgusted, Mallory moved back to her earlier spot against the wall. A late model sedan cruised by, but she wasn't about to bite. Not even Shay would drive that conservatively, she thought. The motorcyclist behind it apparently agreed, whipping out to pass it on the right, and pull up at the curb. The rider flipped up his visor. "Hop on," Shay said.

Mallory blinked and pushed away from the wall. It wasn't often that people surprised her. "Nice bike," she said, admiring the gleaming chrome and black paint. "You know, I was taking bets with myself on what kind of vehicle you'd drive."

"Really." He reached behind him and handed her a helmet. "And what did you decide?"

"I figured you'd show up in something witheringly practical like a station wagon." Mallory pulled her hair back and slid the fiberglass shell over her head.

"In a city with very little parking, a motorcycle *is* practical."

"You sure that it's not just a little bit of Shay's wild side trying to get out?" she asked, straddling the bike.

He turned and gave her a smile that had her pulse speeding up a bit. "You're just dying to turn me into a bad boy, aren't you?"

She wrapped her arms around him, luxuriating in the solid strength of his torso. "Didn't you know? That's what we bad girls do."

His bark of laughter disappeared in the rev of the engine. He flipped down his visor. "Well hold on, because we're heading out."

It had been years since she'd been on the back of a bike, but the exhilaration came back almost immediately: the heat and throb of the engine between her legs, the feel of the wind whipping her face. She was vividly conscious of the feel of Shay's body against her, the heat of his narrow hips between her legs.

To her disappointment, though, he didn't head out

of town or drive along the shoreline highway. Instead he threaded his way through the narrow streets lined with two and three story colonial buildings that made up the heart of Newport's old town. They held the predictable B&B's, antiques stores and galleries, but also flats, launderettes and hardware stores.

He paused at a light, and pulled onto Bellevue Avenue. She'd heard about this part of town; it was impossible to be in Newport and *not* hear about Bellevue Avenue. Fall mums in bronze and gold spilled out of planters in front of the handful of exclusive shops that lined the opening blocks. Ahead of them, the broad road stretched into a residential area, protected with high brick walls on either side, oaks and maples marching along it in a glorious flood of fall color.

But it wasn't the shops or the trees that made Bellevue Avenue special. Once, during the Gilded Age, New York society families fueled by railroad and shipping fortunes fled to Newport to escape the sweltering Manhattan summers. In their cottages by the sea, they'd enjoy the breezes and the summer social season. Of course, some of those cottages, she'd heard, had cost millions of dollars, built at a time when a man might labor all day to earn two.

And they were built as solidly as man could make. Nearly a century later, many of them still stood, palatial and resplendent behind their gated walls. Some were private homes or museums; others played host to a steady stream of visitors hoping to recapture some of the beauty and grace of a time gone by.

"Good Lord." Mallory practically broke her neck staring at an enormous Baroque town house that stretched a block and easily soared forty or fifty feet high. The owners didn't bother with anything so practical as a brick wall. Instead a wrought-iron fence some eight or ten feet high stretched in front of it so all could see its carved stone glory. Urns as tall as a man flanked the steps to the pillared entrance area, late mums spilling out over the top. It took very little effort to imagine carriages pulling up the broad sweep of the entrance driveway to drop the cream of New York society for dinners and balls.

On the other side of the street, they passed a field-stone Gothic revival that looked like something out of *Jane Eyre*. She could imagine an imperiled heroine in love with the master, every bit as much as she could imagine an insane relation locked up in the attic. Around the outside marched formal gardens with hedges and reflecting pools; in an elite town like Newport, these acres of open space were perhaps the biggest extravagance of all.

They passed mansion after mansion marked with the banners of the Newport Historical Society. A person could spend days seeing them all, Mallory thought in wonder. The first fall leaves made bright spots of color on the pavement ahead of them as Shay wove his way along a side street to the highest wall, the grandest gates she'd seen yet. He stopped the bike in a parking area and Mallory got off, her legs still vibrating a little from the engine. The crashing of ocean waves sounded in the distance.

"Did people really used to live in places like this?" she asked, pulling off the helmet and shaking her hair out.

"They still do. Take a drive through Bel Air or Grosse Point some time."

"So is this history lesson day?"

Shay pulled the bike up onto its kickstand and got

off. "If you like. We were talking about tradition yesterday. I thought you might like to see some of it up close." He led her across the street through the enormous stone arches that protected the drive. Ornate wrought iron gates twice as tall as a man stood open in welcome; in the pattern, a script D and V intertwined.

"What does DV stand for?" she asked as they stood in line at the ticket kiosk.

"DeVasher. They made a fortune in railroads and canal boats. Mama DeVasher was a New York society dragon, so when she decided to build a house up here for the summer season, everything had to be bigger and better than anyone else's."

And it was indeed bigger and better. The wide cobblestone driveway curved in from the imposing gates, leading to an enormous stone house that rose high overhead to a rounded cap roof of copper that glowed bluish-green.

Mallory glanced at him as they walked toward the front door. "Do you think the staff here went to O'Connor's for a pint when they got off work?"

"Maybe some. From what I understand, the families usually brought along their normal butlers and cooks, but some of the groundskeepers and chambermaids were probably local."

"So some of the money from the idle rich here eventually found its way into your great grampa's pocket. You could consider yourselves beneficiaries of the DeVasher family."

"History has a million stories."

Mallory sighed, looking at the sweep of the driveway and a courtyard that could have housed a football field. "Yeah, well I expect the people who lived here had the best of it."

"Don't be so sure," Shay disagreed. "From what I understand, they actually had it pretty tough. One son died of smallpox, another in a freak carriage accident. Their twins died when the Titanic went down, and the great flu epidemic took a couple more. Even Daddy DeVasher only lived about six months after the house was done. He stayed here once."

"You think being poor with your family around you would be better?"

His nod was quick and certain. "Absolutely. You can always make more money. You can't replace family. It's fundamental."

Mallory gave a derisive snort. "I think you've led a very sheltered life."

He studied her. "Or maybe you've led a challenging one."

"Nothing worth talking about," she said lightly, "so don't waste your time asking."

"You might just find it worth talking about one of these days," he said slowly, locking eyes with her.

For a heartbeat, she couldn't look away. Then the moment passed and she shook her head briskly. "Don't bet on it, pal." Sex and sex alone, she thought. She was the only person she needed inside her head.

They stopped to stare out over the emerald-green lawn that framed the house, and to the blue sea beyond. "How many people do you think it took to run a place like this?" Mallory asked idly.

Shay flicked a glance at her that was as blue as the waves beyond them. "I think it was forty or fifty by the time you count the outdoors and the stables. The house covers something like an acre."

"It would have been like a little city, with its own rules and pecking order," she mused. "Have you ever seen any of the old costume dramas, where all the servants were called by the name of whoever they served, like in *Gosford Park?* There'd have been all sorts of little intrigues and jealousies going on. Imagine, an illicit affair between the coachman and the girl who ironed the sheets."

He raised an eyebrow. "Ironed the sheets?"

Mallory drew herself up and looked down her nose at him. "Eunice DeVasher does not sleep on unpressed sheets, Worthington. If your coachman continues to trifle with my maid and interfere with her work, I shall be forced to make mention of it. I suggest that you see to your staff, sir."

"I am the butler, Mrs. Tibbets," Shay returned in an equally snotty tone. "Such outdoor services are below my notice. The housekeeping staff is your duty, madam, and I suggest you see to it."

"Don't presume to tell me my duties, sir."

"Nor you, me."

Mallory laughed in delight as they began walking again, past the formal gardens that led to the front door. "She'd have worn discreet skirts and pulled her hair back into this tight little bun without a single hair escaping."

Shay grinned at her. "He'd have worn a suit without a single wrinkle or speck of dust, and his hair slicked back within an inch of its life."

"And of course you know there would have been all that repressed sexual desire between the two of them the whole time they were sniping." She walked through the door he held open for her.

"Power is an aphrodisiac," Shay said as they followed the guard's direction to join the tour group at the end of the entrance hall. "Running the house for a powerful family would have been power by proxy."

"When you're controlling fifty people, it's not proxy at all. It's real powe—good God." Mallory stopped. They stood at the point where the main hallway opened into the central atrium of the building. Sheets of green and gray marble sheathed walls that rose sixty feet to the gold-leafed crown moldings. The ceiling soared overhead, painted with puffy clouds on which Greek gods dressed in togas reclined.

Dressed in a sweater, skirt, and sensible heels, the guide cleared her throat and began her cool, practiced pitch. "The Shoreline is a Renaissance revival building. Note the ceiling, which depicts Zeus, Apollo and Artemis."

Mallory leaned toward Shay. "Where's Eros?" she whispered in his ear.

"On the ceiling of Mr. DeVasher's bedroom."

Mallory snorted a laugh.

They followed the tour along the grand staircase to the upper floor, past an enormous Greek-style tapestry. Commodore DeVasher stared down at them imposingly from a portrait on the wall, his epaulets and gold buttons gleaming.

"The Commodore has complained of fingerprints on his buttons, Mrs. Tibbets. Please take care that the laundry staff shines them properly."

"I suggest that the fault lies with the person hanging them up, Worthington," she returned. "The buttons are perfectly polished when they leave our laundry room."

"The Commodore's room," the guide announced, leading them into a space Mallory calculated was roughly twice the size of her entire apartment. DeVasher had liked surrounding himself with luxury, she thought, staring at the heavy, dark walnut furniture. The old-fashioned carved four-poster bed sat up on a dais as though DeVasher were emperor of all he surveyed. And so, in this place, he was, she supposed.

The tour guide waved the group along. "And here is the DeVashers' shared bathroom. You can see the marble tub that was the Commodore's favorite."

Fashioned with carved columns and acanthus leaves along the outside, the translucent marble tub was about eight feet long and big enough for two. "Now that's a bathtub," Mallory said reverently. All it needed to be perfect was champagne, the warm light of afternoon sun shining in the windows, and a pair of slippery, naked bathers. "Do you think Worthington and Mrs. Tibbets ever sneaked in while the DeVashers were away?" she whispered in Shay's ear.

Shay coughed and they followed the tour group into Mrs. DeVasher's private space. If the Commodore's room was luxurious, Mrs. DeVasher's was frankly opulent. Lace streamed down from the half tester to drape over a bed piled with fringed satin pillows. Faded tapestries in muted pastels covered the walls, silk draperies framed the windows. On the marble mantle sat a Fabergé egg.

Mallory leaned closer to Shay. "I bet the Commodore liked to hang out in the bathroom with the door open just a crack and watch Mrs. DeVasher undress."

"You think?"

"Oh, yes, and then he'd sneak in the room like an intruder and toss her down on the bed and ravish her."

Shay regarded her with interest. "Do you think society matrons liked to be ravished?"

Mallory sent him a look from under her lashes. "Sweet pea, every woman likes to be ravished."

He held her eyes for just a beat, his stare full of helpless heat. Then the tour guide led them out of the bedroom and back downstairs.

"Do you want to walk out over the grounds?" Shay asked when they were finished.

"Wouldn't miss it," she said following him.

The wide swath of lawn galloped from the back porch of the house toward the water, separated from the blue of the sea and the tumble of boulders along the shore by a waist high wall of carved marble.

"So do you think that eventually Worthington and Mrs. Tibbets broke down and gave in to their mad attraction?" Shay asked as they wandered up to the marble wall.

"People generally do," she said, her eyes lingering on him for a beat before she turned to stare at the waves beyond.

"They would have had a lot to lose," he observed, watching her profile.

"Eventually you hit a point where that doesn't matter anymore, don't you Shay?" Her eyes locked with his and he felt it like a punch in his gut. He didn't want to want her, he had a lot to lose over it, but he wondered how long he could hold out before he hit that point where it didn't matter to him, either.

Mallory raked her hair back and leaned against the fence to look back at the house.

"It would make you different to live this way, don't you think?" She narrowed her eyes at the palace in front of them. "Actually I expect that after a while the reality of having that much money would make you a little barmy. Especially if all you did was lay around and get waited on hand and foot.''

"I doubt they ever thought about it." It interested him that she did, though.

"Maybe not consciously, but I think everybody has a need to be productive."

"It depends on how you define productive. Back then, if you threw a good party you were toasted as a hugely successful society hostess. Even if all you did was approve the menus and preside graciously over the whole thing.''

Mallory pushed her hair back out of her eyes. Shay struggled not to remember how it had felt in his hands.

"I think doing nothing would still make me feel shiftless," she argued. "And the idea of having live-in servants... I mean, don't get me wrong, I'd be thrilled if I never had to clean house or cook again, but the idea of having people constantly in the house would make me crazy. How could you live without privacy?''

The sea breeze carried more than just a salt tang. It carried her scent. "I don't imagine the DeVashers and their guests even noticed them. They'd grown up with servants, remember.''

"How can you ignore a living, breathing person? Could you? So what if I were trotting around in a maid's outfit. I wouldn't be any less there.''

Unbidden, an image bloomed in Shay's mind of Mallory dressed as a saucy French maid, in short black dress with a little white apron. "Servants back then were taught to be invisible.''

She eyed him. "I don't think I'd be very good at that.''

"I don't think you would be, either," he agreed.

How could she be invisible when he saw her even in his dreams? She was the sort of woman a man would lose his head over, the kind the gentleman of the house would risk everything to have.

Mallory rose on tiptoe to look over the thick wall at the footpath that wound along its base, seven or eight feet below them. "So what's that?" she asked, spying a narrow, meandering path with her eyes.

"The Cliff Walk. It winds along the coast for a mile or two. They used to promenade along it back in the day."

"Can we go down there?"

Don't go, he lectured himself. The key was to keep in public, to keep his distance, to keep his head, so the wanting wouldn't take him over.

"Please?" she asked again, her eyes bright. "I love the ocean."

"Okay," he said before he could stop himself. "We're right by an entry point."

She linked her fingers with him to pull him away from the wall. "Take me there," she demanded.

MALLORY STOOD ON THE NARROW trail that wound between the jagged coastal rocks on one side and the mansions on the other, listening to the rush and flow of the water. Waves hit rhythmically, tossing up spume. Shore birds cried out as they circled overhead. On her right, on the inland side, late summer wild flowers still bloomed and green lawns rolled away to impossibly large mansions. To her left, was a poetic violence of pounding surf.

Something about the ocean had always called to her. One of the few bright spots growing up had been the occasional trips to the Jersey shore. Staring at the waves, watching their ebb and flow, she'd dreamed about freedom.

Now, years later, Mallory took a deep breath and savored the briny scent. "I can't believe I didn't know about this," she said, threading her way along the deserted path, following the trail to where it dipped toward a pedestrian tunnel that cut through a rocky outcrop.

"I come down here a lot when I need to clear out my head and think. Is this your first time to the shore since you've been here?" Shay held back and let her go ahead of him, dragging his eyes up from the leggy litheness of her walk.

She nodded. "I've been down at the waterfront, obviously, but not to the real coast. I've been pretty busy. I needed this, though," she said, sucking in a deep breath of ocean air. "Being by the sea always makes me feel, I don't know…recharged, I guess. Like something I didn't know was missing got refilled. Maybe I was a sea witch in a previous life or something." Mallory laughed and glanced back over her shoulder to Shay and just for a moment something tightened painfully in him. Her eyes were witchy dark, strands of her hair dancing around her face in the breeze. The curve of her mouth could certainly bewitch a man; maybe it had already bewitched him.

He'd braced himself from the beginning to ignore what her face and body did to him. It was a low blow that the truest seduction was coming from her mind, from listening to her husky mellow voice as they walked down the isolated path.

"So how did you wind up in bartending? Why not college?"

Mallory shrugged. "I'd rather study what interests

me than what people tell me I should. Besides, who could afford it?''

"There are a lot of things in between, though." The trail widened out so they could walk side by side. Ahead of them, the tunnel neared.

"Bartending is a good job for a person who has itchy feet. There are always plenty of jobs in every city, so it's easy to move on." She gave him a side-long glance. "It probably seems strange to you. You've lived here all your life, haven't you?''

Shay nodded. His life had been built on the solid absolutes of family and home. There was a sense of history, both global and personal, in every day, in every street he walked down. There was something strangely alluring about the idea of living in a place where every corner of every street was an invitation to a new adventure. The part of him that had felt increasingly stifled of late wondered what it would be like to just strike out, try something different, something unexpected. Someone unexpected.

Like Mallory.

"You're awfully quiet."

He shook his head to banish the thought. "I was just trying to imagine what it would be like, driving into a town I didn't know from anywhere and setting up shop."

She considered. "It's a mix. Exciting, because everything is new and you don't know what's going to happen. A little frustrating because you don't know any of the things people take for granted, like where to find the post office or drugstore or bank." She bounced her fist lightly on the waist-high ledge of concrete that ran on the inland side of the walk. "Exhilarating, because it's a fresh start and great things could be coming your way.''

They stepped into the pedestrian tunnel, an arch of corrugated iron. It curved part way through, cutting off the light and blocking their view of the tunnel ahead. "With all the new, though, do you ever miss the old?" Shay asked, his voice echoing down the long tube.

Mallory's laugh sounded oddly intimate in the enclosed space. "With all of the old, do you ever miss something new?" She stumbled on a rough bit of footing in the dim light and clutched at his arm for support. When she'd steadied herself, she didn't let go. Awareness spread through him.

He tried to focus on her question as they rounded the bend in the tunnel, anything to keep from thinking about touching her more. "I think everyone gets restless sometimes," he said. The sound of the waves grew louder as they neared the mouth.

Mallory stopped, her feet in sunlight, her face in shadow. Her eyes were dark, her voice close as she reached out to brush a stray lock of hair out of his eyes. "Is that what you are now, Shay? Restless?" Her touch shivered over him. "Welcome to my world," she murmured. Then she flowed up against him and swept his senses into overload.

Hot and sweet, her mouth was avid on his, tempting him to taste, then taste deeper still. Satisfaction had nothing to do with it—every stroke, every touch, every brush of her lips made him crave more. The rhythm of her kiss was the rhythm of sex, and he found himself moving against her without realizing it. She was all slender strength in his arms. The soft murmur she made in her throat had the blood roaring in his ears.

This was what he wanted, not just the mouth and the body but the person. It was all wound together inextricably in a vortex of desire that pulled him in. Outside the tunnel, waves crashed against the rocks and the breeze sent dead leaves scudding and scraping against the paved Cliff Walk. Inside, there was only Mallory. Sleek and fragrant, she pulled him into a private world of sensuality where only the physical dominated.

His hands roved over her body, feeling the slender strength of it, molding her against him. It made him dizzy, it made him hard, it sent his pulse rocketing to feel her shiver at his touch as he slid his hand under her coat, under her sweater. If he could just touch her skin, he told himself, it would be enough. If he could just feel that satiny texture, the solid fullness of her breasts, he could stop.

Mallory gave a soft groan at his touch, turning so he could reach her more easily. This was what she needed, the heat of his hands on her. She reached up to guide his fingers to the clasp of her bra and a flood of arousal flowed through her as the soft friction of his fingers brushed against the sensitive skin. He squeezed her nipple and a thousand nerve endings exploded, sending bolts of desire through to the center of her. Oh, the heat of his hands wasn't enough, she needed more.

Voices suddenly echoed through the tunnel. Shay cursed and jerked back, breathing hard. The rush of cool air after the heat of his touch had goosebumps forming on her skin. For an instant, all she could do was feel. Then she blinked and swiftly slid her bra back into place, the friction of the fabric dragging awareness from her already sensitized nipples.

Without a word, Shay turned and led her back into the tunnel. Mallory headed after him, her fingers rubbing her lips almost absently. The acoustics were deceiving; the group that they'd heard was only just stepping into the tunnel as they neared the mouth. Still, Shay said nothing, only reaching out to help her once when she stumbled.

They stepped out of the echoing tunnel and onto the deserted Cliff Walk. Shay just kept walking, and annoyance swept through her. "Look, don't go getting angry at me. You were into that as much as I was."

"I'm not angry at you," he said shortly. "I'm angry at myself."

"Why? We're consenting adults, Shay, and we both want it."

He raked his fingers through his hair in exasperation. "Jesus, Mallory, I'm trying to do the right thing here."

"The right thing according to who?" Her voice rose. "What, did you make a pact with my brother that you wouldn't touch me no matter what?"

He rounded on her. "No, but I told him I'd take care of you, and in guy speak that doesn't mean sleeping with a guy's sister."

She gave him a cool look. "Then I guess you've got yourself a choice, Shay," she purred. "You can either do what your head tells you to do or you can do what you think you should do, or go ahead and do what you want to do."

"I generally try to live my life so that what I want to do *is* what I should do."

"You know, Shay, you've got yourself trapped in this Mr. Upright persona when there's this whole other side to you begging to get out. You're restless? Of course you're restless, you want to be human for a change. That's a new Harley you brought me here on.'' She gave him a speculative look. ''I'd say you were too young for a midlife crisis, except that it sounds like you've been holding up the responsibilities of a grown man since you were a teenager.'' Impatient, she strode up to him and kissed him, hard. ''I want you, Shay,'' she said simply, running her fingers up his chest. ''And you want me. What does Dev matter? How would he even know?''

''I'd know.''

''Haven't you been getting tired of being the good one? You've always been the good boy, the one who was dependable, who never got a chance to say what the hell. Isn't it time, Shay?'' Her voice was soft, hypnotic. ''Time you said what the hell and did what felt good without worrying about the consequences? Loosen the leash for a change. Do something irresponsible.''

''Like break my word to your brother?''

Mallory held his eye for a moment, then shook her head. ''Have it your way. Just don't expect me to make it any easier on you because I know what we both want.''

''I already know enough about you not to expect easy.''

She curled her hand into the front of his shirt and pulled him close. ''For you, Shay, I'm a pushover.''

7

A BREATH OF EARLY FALL chill lingered in the evening air as they walked from the dark parking lot toward the bright lights of the roadhouse. A doorman sat in the garish glow of the neon sign; cars whipped by periodically on the highway.

"Ernie's Hideaway?" Shay read dubiously.

"Hey, what do you want? We're here to audition a bar band, not U2," Mallory said, shifting the small bag that she had looped across her bandolero-style.

Jukebox rock flowed out into the darkness along with the scent of cigarettes and the sound of laughter. "Cover's five bucks a head, man." The bearded doorman held his hand out to Shay, but his eyes lingered on Mallory.

Shay gave the doorman a ten.

"Have a good time," he said, turning around on his stool to watch Mallory as they walked in.

She gave him a careless smile that had his heart palpitating, then turned to Shay. "Paying my way?" she asked with an ironic lift to her eyebrow. "Watch out, you'll get me thinking we are on a date."

The smile that seemed to perpetually hover around the corners of her mouth bloomed then, making his pulse bump. A date? In his dreams, which she had begun to haunt on a nightly basis. Unfortunately she was off limits, a fact his mind understood but his body refused to accept.

"We're doing this for your bar," he said, giving her a look. "You should be paying for me."

She blew him a kiss. "How about if I buy you a drink, instead, big boy?" she asked playfully and turned to plunge into the dimness of Ernie's.

Located on a highway outside of Newport, it was more a roadhouse than a club. The walls were a scarred beige, unadorned except for a tattered poster of Spuds McKenzie next to the darts board. Plain planked wood covered the floor. The establishment flowed from the main bar area to an area with billiards and shuffleboard, to an area where the bands played. The bandstand was currently empty of people except for someone who was either a roadie or a musician fiddling with an amp.

Shay followed Mallory as she wandered idly. Most people entered a bar and gravitated to get a drink then find someplace they could make into their comfort zone. Mallory seemed to have no such compulsion. She strolled, relaxed and curious, scoping out the bar, stepping around the dance floor, studying the place like a cat exploring a new home.

And everywhere she went, men watched her. She wore a narrow red silk minidress that showcased long, sleek legs in matching stilettos. The halter neckline dipped low and left her shoulders bare. Her hair was a wild tumble of sable.

She walked blithely past men who tried to catch her eye with a smile. Her lack of reaction made it easier for Shay to stifle the sudden surge of protectiveness. He would have done a better job of convincing himself that he felt it on behalf of her brother if it hadn't been for the way the silky curve of her hip begged for the touch of his hands.

Mallory turned and gave him a glance, then, as though she knew where he'd been looking. "You want to get a drink?"

"Sure."

At the bar, they'd barely found themselves stools before the bartender stood in front of them. "What'll you have?" he asked. One of the advantages of being out with a beautiful woman, Shay reflected, was that you were seldom invisible.

Mallory touched the tip of her tongue to her upper lip and suddenly every molecule of Shay's body was hummingly aware of her. "Maker's Mark, on the rocks," she said finally, with a smile that probably made the bartender's night.

As Shay ordered a Dewar's, Mallory turned to lean against the wooden bar and stare out into the room.

Shay turned around to follow her gaze. "So what, you thinking to add Spuds McKenzie to your decor?"

"It's hard to stop working," she said. "I'm always curious to see what people seem to like."

"And what do people here seem to like?" The jukebox was loud enough he had to lean close to her to be heard.

She turned to pick up her drink and threw him a smile. "Same thing they always have, pretty much. Drinks, pool, music. Flirting with the opposite sex." She dipped a finger in her bourbon to stir it, then and put it in her mouth to suck it dry. "Especially flirting."

Knowing she was fully aware of the effect she was having on him didn't stop his system from responding.

"You broke a couple of hearts earlier when you didn't react." He sipped from his own drink.

She raised an eyebrow as she paid the bartender. "Did you want me to?"

He hadn't, Shay realized with sudden intensity. "As your brother-appointed chaperone, I probably shouldn't encourage it."

"I'm sure my brother knows I talk to men occasionally."

"Trust me, it's something brothers don't like to think about."

She leaned over so close to him that her lips just brushed his ear. "Shay, when are you going to stop being the responsible guy and start letting yourself enjoy life a little?"

Wanting what he couldn't have, what he shouldn't have was driving him slowly mad. Irritation surged through him. "Don't be so sure you've got me figured out," he said abruptly, trying to ignore her scent. "I'm not nearly as simple as you think."

Her eyes darkened. "Does that mean that if I tempt you too much you might bend me over a table and ravish me?"

The image, the way it would feel, bloomed in his mind. It had been hard enough to pull back the previous day when she was fully clothed and in cool and breezy daylight. Now, in a warm, dark bar, all he could think was that he wanted to make her his.

"So you really didn't do the bar thing when you were younger, did you?" she asked him curiously.

"I worked in a bar nearly every night. The last thing I wanted to do when I had a night off was go into another one."

"Must have limited your dating repertoire."

"Life limited my dating repertoire," he said lightly, watching a guy across the room teaching a giggling girl how to shoot pool. "When you're twenty-two or twenty-three, most women expect to go out on the weekends, especially if they've got a boyfriend. Tuesday night just isn't the same."

Mallory crossed her legs, sending his thoughts scattering. "Well, maybe we should pretend this is a date, just so you can get back some of your young adulthood. To going back in time." She clicked her glass against his.

Shay looked at her speculatively as he let the scotch slide over his tongue. "What about you?"

"What do you mean, what about me?"

"When did you start bartending?"

She flicked a glance at him, then looked out across the room. "As soon as I was legal. I started out cocktail waitressing in a bowling alley. The bartender got sick one night, so they put me back there."

"You must have been a quick study."

"It's not exactly rocket science," she said dryly. "Besides, they had pretty simple tastes. His bartending book gave me enough to get started."

"So you couldn't have had a whole lot more opportunities to go out than I did."

"Don't you worry about me, Shay. I had plenty of chances to kick up my heels." She gave him a bawdy wink. "I'm the original bad girl, remember?"

"So you're always telling me."

Mallory looked toward the bandstand, where the musicians were picking up their instruments. "Looks like the Blues Jockeys are getting ready to play."

He winced. "The Blues Jockeys?"

Mallory laughed at his pained expression. "They're a bar band, cut 'em some slack."

"Let me guess, they play jazz."

"Perish the thought. I want stuff you can get hot and sweaty to." She traced her fingertips over the back of his hand in a teasing brush. "That's what I like when I'm dancing. What about you, Shay?"

A twang of a guitar string and thump of a bass drum saved him from answering. With a click from the drummer, the band launched into a cover of "Mony Mony."

Mallory listened for a few minutes, moving her shoulders to the beat. "Okay, they're not going to light up the planet with creativity, but they're all right. What do you think?"

The alluring cleft that appeared between her breasts every time she shifted a shoulder forward made it hard to concentrate on the music. Shay gathered his scrambled thoughts. "Nothing wrong with a cover band for bar music. It would be nice to hear something that's not a wedding reception standard, though."

"Kind of my thought, too," she admitted. "I guess the question is do they get people onto the dance floor? That's the key. People dance, they get thirsty and they buy drinks."

He gave her an appraising glance. "Don't miss a trick, do you?"

"Not when I'm playing with somebody else's money, I don't."

The song changed to an infectious groove that had him bouncing his heel lightly on the ground and moving his shoulders. "Better," he nodded.

"Would you dance to it?"

"I might," he decided. "How about you?"

''Definitely.'' She stood up. ''Let's go.''

Over on the dance floor, everything was louder. In an open spot up by the stage, Mallory turned and started swaying to the music. The beat was hypnotic. It vibrated through Shay's system until he was keeping time. Then she began to seriously move and he forgot everything but the rhythm pounding in his head and the woman in front of him.

It was less a dance than a seduction. Running her fingers back through her thick curtain of hair and looking at him through slumberous eyes, she had the look of a woman welcoming her lover to her bed. Her hips moved sinuously, snapping on the beat in a darkly sexy cadence. Her arms flowed through the air to the music, now snapping to it, now tracing their way up her body. She wove the same spell as she had when she'd been up on the bar. Except that this time she was in front of him, just a foot away. And as more people crowded the dance floor, the distance narrowed.

Shay stepped closer and Mallory took his hand to spin in against him, her back to him, his arms wrapped around her. The scent of her hair, the feel of her curves under his hands sent his system into overload. Then she turned to face him, fragrant and smooth. And then quickly, he felt himself grow rock hard.

There was no point in trying to hide it. Eyes dark, she pressed herself to him, still moving to the music, tantalizing him more with every sway of her hips. Each push against him, each brush of heat and warmth jolted through his muscles. His hands slid around her waist, pulling her in tighter. He was long past even thinking about holding back.

When she brushed her mouth against his, it seemed only an extension of the dance, less a temptation than a physical imperative. The touch of her body, the touch of her lips blended together in a flush of sensation. It was more like making love than dancing. Desire rippled through him. He could feel her breasts against him, warm and yielding. He could feel her fingers playing down his back, slipping under the waistband of his jeans.

The crowd around them receded from his awareness, the music no longer even registered except as something to drive their motion. The only thing real was Mallory against him, pliant and eager. Mallory was the only thing that mattered, the only thing he wanted.

"Shay." She stopped kissing him long enough to breathe his name over his lips.

"What?"

"Let's go. Now."

They stopped to kiss outside of the bar. Shay could hear the throb of the music through the walls, could feel the throb of sex running through his veins. Control was gone, he was saturated by desire.

In the dark of the back parking lot, urgency compelled him to drag her close and feast on her mouth. *Now, now, now* drummed insistently through his bloodstream. He straddled the bike and pulled on his gloves. Then Mallory melted into his arms.

"Don't wait," she whispered, "here."

He felt her hands unbuttoning the front of his shirt and slipping in to stroke his chest, pinch the nipples lightly. Then her other slid out to stroke his thighs, the heat of her fingers coming through the denim of his jeans.

A car rushed by out on the highway, but the parking lot was silent, everyone inside dancing to the band.

Now, he thought. Dev didn't matter, responsibility didn't matter, nothing mattered but that he should silence this desire that was slowly driving him mad.

THE HARD, SMOOTH PLANES of his chest, the parallel ridges of his abs quivered under her fingers. It was irresistible. She wanted to be licking them, tasting them, laying against him skin to skin. She wanted to see him naked, then touch all of him.

Mallory could feel him shuddering against her fingers. Wondering what it would feel like to make love with him made a jolt of anticipation run through her. Knowing that his desire for her had brought them to this point was intoxicating. *Soon,* she thought, almost unable to breathe for the desire clogging her lungs. His arm wrapped around her to pull her close, onto the seat in front of him.

She'd thought about sex with him for nearly a week, teased him, goaded him, urged him on. Now, it seemed, his inhibitions were gone. She'd unleashed a different Shay, one driven by desire. Gone were any attempts to hold back. Instead he pushed her relentlessly, pushed them both. His hands were hard and urgent on her, his mouth demanding a response.

Mallory tangled her fingers in his hair and pressed his mouth harder against hers. Once, she'd aimed them toward this moment with a goal in mind. Now, the act itself was the only thing that mattered. Friction, pressure and heat fused together in one inextricable tangle of sensation, until her entire being focused on the connection of their lips.

Oh, but there was more. The touch of his fingers in their leather riding gloves tantalized and aroused as they slipped up her sides, but then he made a muffled noise of impatience and stripped them off. Then it was just the heat of his hands against her skin.

He skimmed the tip of his tongue down her throat as he untied her halter top and the red dress fell away. She let her head fall back against the arm supporting her. His other hand, his clever fingers, searched out the front clasp of her bra and flicked it open. She helped him pull the stretchy red fabric out of the way.

The low, involuntary sound she made, not quite a groan, was one Shay echoed as his hand slid up over her bare breast. The slight roughness of his palm teased, the warmth inflamed. Then he began concentrating on her nipple, spiraling in toward it, brushing it, squeezing it until she was riding the delicious knife edge of pleasure and pain. She did groan then, in surrender, in anticipation.

Anticipation was what drove Shay, as he leaned down to lick at her nipples, feeling her shudder at the sensation. He knew she could feel, had to feel his cock straining against the denim of his jeans. In the faint light of the parking lot, her aureoles showed as dark smudges on the pale fullness of her breasts.

He bent his head and his mouth was on her, sucking first one, then the other nipple. There was something primal about it, the feeling of that hard nub against his tongue, against his lips. There was something immensely arousing in hearing her soft cry.

Then she was pushing his head away, standing up and reaching down to unfasten his jeans. In rapid succession he felt the shock of night air on his cock, then the bigger shock of the heat of her hand.

Mallory laughed softly and gave him a stroke that had his breath hissing in. "No underwear, Shay? You *are* walking on the wild side." She moved her hand, then ran her finger up to the tip of him where he could feel the pearly drop of precome that had slipped out. She slid her fingertip down the length of his hard-on, spreading the slippery fluid and leaving a trail of frenzied nerve endings in her wake.

Then she raised her fingertip up to her lips and sucked on it, as she'd done before with the bourbon. ''Mmm, I think I need a better taste.'' She knelt down beside him and slipped him into the wet heat of her mouth, and the world turned into a single spot of blinding pleasure.

The sound of Shay's helpless groan sounded in Mallory's ears as she moved her mouth up and down the hard length of him. There was something incredibly arousing about the immediacy of giving pleasure that generated such an obvious response. She moved her head, the silky smooth skin tightened against her lips. She stroked with her tongue, he caught his breath. She sucked, and she could feel his body tense as he fought for control.

Then his fingers were pulling at her shoulders to raise her.

''No,'' she protested. ''I want to…''

''Now,'' he said raggedly. ''I need to be in you now.'' Then he cursed.

''What?'' she asked, fumbling in the pouch at her hip.

''We don't have a condom.''

''Oh, yes, we do,'' she breathed pulling one out of her bag. ''Don't miss a trick, I believe you said?'' The plastic crackled. Mallory leaned in for a kiss and threw a leg over the bike so that she straddled Shay, her legs atop his. He pushed the silky dress up to her hips. She felt his palms run over her thighs. Then he slid them underneath her and helped her rise.

"Mmm, now who's living on the wild side?" he murmured as his fingers slid over the bare skin under her skirt.

Mallory moaned a little at the slippery smooth feel of the head of his cock as she rubbed it against the slick cleft between her legs. Then he put his hands on her hips and pulled her down. And all she could do was clutch blindly at his shoulders and cry out at the slippery friction as he impaled her on him.

His hands were strong around her ribs, holding her, helping her move. His flesh pulsed hard and hot inside her. Every stroke sent shivers racing through her. Every stroke, he went so deep that pleasure and pain blurred into one overwhelming surge of sensation that had her fighting not to cry out. The sliding, tormenting friction pulled her nearer and nearer to orgasm until she tumbled over, moaning and jolting against him. And an instant later, he followed.

THE SECONDS TICKED BY as their heart rates slowed. Mallory leaned bonelessly against Shay, feeling his breath on her hair. The sound of a car passing on the highway registered only dimly.

"Mal," Shay said softly.

"Hmm?"

"We're in the parking lot. We have to get ourselves fixed up and home."

She opened her eyes then. It took all the energy she had to straighten up. "I suppose you're right."

He reached out to help her fasten her bra and pull her top down, his hands brushing over her bare breasts as he did.

Desire sliced through her as if the previous few moments had never happened. Oh, yes, they did need to get home. And then they needed to get naked and do it all over again.

She braced herself and slid off Shay, the smooth, intimate rush of skin against skin making her catch her breath again. When he handed her her helmet, she leaned in for a kiss instead and they lost long minutes to the addictive taste of mouth against mouth.

Finally she straddled the bike behind him and then they were riding down the back road through the night.

MALLORY STOOD IN THE ALLEYWAY behind her apartment, watching Shay pull his bike up onto the kick stand. He pulled off his helmet and got off the bike himself.

She stepped in to kiss him. "Let's go inside," she breathed. "I've got plans for you." She tugged at his hand to lead him toward her back stairs.

At the top, she unlocked the door that let them into her kitchen. Then she started to pull off his jacket. Shay shook his head and closed his hands over hers.

"We need to talk."

"What about?"

He looked at her. "What we're doing here. What to tell your brother, for a start."

Her chin came up a little at that. "The same thing I usually tell him when I sleep with someone. Nothing." Dev was the last person she wanted to be thinking about just then. In fact, just then she really didn't want to think too much about anything.

Except the way it had felt to be with Shay.

She fought off impatience. This wasn't the way it was supposed to go. This wasn't the way it was sup-

posed to go at all. No involvement. The plan had been
to get him to sleep with her so that he'd make tracks
the other way. She'd thought she'd known how he'd
react, but that was before a wholly unexpected Shay
emerged. She thought she'd wanted to get rid of him;
now need for him overwhelmed her. It was just sex,
she reminded herself. Nice, mindless sex.

She started to walk past him to the living room,
snapping a switch to turn on soft lighting from a lamp
in the corner.

"I don't care whether you usually talk to Dev or
not." Shay followed her into a room of plush furniture
and warm wood. "I think this is a little different and
we need to figure out what just happened."

She turned to face him, leaning against the bur-
gundy velvet sofa. "No one ever told you about the
birds and bees?" she asked. "I'll give you another
lesson, if you like."

Shay followed her. "Not until I know what's going
on here."

"What's going on here is sex," she said, with a bit
more emphasis than she'd planned. "It's got nothing
to do with Dev or business or anything else. Just you
and me. In bed."

"I don't usually sleep around just for the hell of
it."

"Well, maybe you should start. Let that wild side
out, Shay," she said softly, moving toward him to
slide her arms around his neck. "Have a secret fling
just for the fun of it. I won't tell if you won't." Just
sex, she thought to herself. And oh, what sex. He
wanted it, she wanted it. That was all she needed to
know.

Her lips were soft against his as she drew him toward the couch. Even as he kissed her back, he hesitated. Finally Mallory pulled back.

"While you deal with your moral quandary, I'm going to give a call downstairs to check on how they're doing. We can have an affair, or you can try to pretend that you don't want it. But decide quick, Shay. I'm not a patient woman." She leaned in for a kiss that was all flash and fire. Before he could react, before his arms could come around her, she disappeared through a doorway at the far side of the room, presumably toward a phone.

Shay sat down slowly on the couch. What to do now, that was the question. He was smart enough to know that there was no way in hell this particular genie was going back in the bottle. There was no point in being ticked off with himself; if he could go back in time, he'd do the same thing. In fact, going back in time didn't sound like such a bad idea. Surely mortal man only got one or two chances at that kind of mind-blowing sex.

Shay scrubbed a hand over his face. There were two possibilities open to him. One was go cold turkey. If he were smart, he'd wash his hands of the whole thing. Tell Mallory so long, tell Dev thanks but no thanks, and get as far and as fast from this mess as he could. Never see that smile ever again. Never touch that soft skin.

Not appealing.

The other option was to say what the hell and take what she was offering. He'd never had a fling in his entire life. In fact, he'd never done anything irresponsible, even. And while he doubted that deep down he was wired for casual sex, now would be the perfect time to find out. Mallory was right, he'd been living too quietly for too long. So they had a blistering affair, so what.

The only problem was that if he was having a blistering affair with Dev's sister, he really had to tell him. It wasn't fair not to. And yet, if he told Dev when Mallory didn't want him to, he'd be betraying her confidence. But if he didn't betray her, he was betraying Dev.

Shay leaned his head back and rubbed his eyes with the heels of his hands. If he were honest, he didn't give a damn about moral quandaries just at the moment. What was hammering through his head above all was the memory of how she had felt against him, how he'd felt inside her. And how much he wanted to feel that again.

He dropped his hands and straightened up.

And his jaw dropped.

Mallory stood looking at him from the doorway to her hall, still wearing her red stilettos.

And absolutely nothing else.

"I thought you needed a little more encouragement," she said softly, walking across the Persian rug toward him. "Does this do the trick, Shay?"

He took two steps toward her and crushed her in his arms.

8

SQUINTING IN THE BRIGHT afternoon sunlight, Mallory pulled the door of Bad Reputation closed and pushed her key into the lock. Especially at times like these, she thought the decision to remain a night time bar was a good one. She fumbled for dark glasses as she heard footsteps behind her on the sidewalk.

"Hey."

Her mouth curved in pleased recognition as she looked over her should to find Shay behind her. "Mmm, and to you, too." She turned to flow in against him for a long, liquid kiss.

It didn't do to think about how good it felt to see him, to have his arms around her again. In the three days since they'd become lovers, Shay had become like some rich, decadent delicacy that she craved incessantly. It was just the novelty of a new lover, that was all, she told herself. A skilled, surprisingly inventive lover, but one who would eventually stop making her pulse throb, as they all did. One who would eventually become possessive and try to reform her.

As they all did.

Now was not the time to think about it, though. Instead she let herself fall into the luxury of his touch, indulging herself in his flavor and scent. Long seconds passed. Finally Mallory broke the kiss and leaned back. "It's been too long since last night."

Shay traced a finger along her cheek. "I seem to recall that you were the one who pushed me out on the street."

Mallory put her head down against his chest. "I told you, I don't sleep well with other people around."

"Sleeping's not what I had in mind." He brushed his lips over her hair. "It's not what I have in mind now."

She softened against him before she remembered her purpose. "I'm afraid you'll have to wait until after closing, big boy."

"Why's that?" His hands were doing tantalizing things to her breasts through the tight T-shirt covering them. What a difference a few days made, Mallory thought. They might have been standing in the doorway niche, but the pride of the Chamber of Commerce was essentially touching her on a street in broad daylight. And oh, what a touch.

She struggled not to go spiraling away to the place he seemed bent on taking her. "I can't do this now. I flubbed up my inventory and we're almost out of cocktail napkins. I've got to go over to the warehouse club to get more."

"There's time," he murmured, bending toward her again.

Mallory slipped neatly out around him. "It's Friday night. I've got to get back here in time to do bar prep." She turned to walk toward her truck, parked farther along the street.

"You can get paper goods delivered, you know," Shay said, catching up to link his fingers with hers as they walked.

"I know, but I get a better price by going to the

warehouse club, believe it or not. Convenience costs money.''

''You use white, right?''

She stopped on the sidewalk by her truck, keys in hand. ''Why do you ask?''

''We just got a delivery of paper goods on Wednesday. I can probably spot you enough to get you by until you have time to go get them. Save you driving over to Providence.''

''Won't that leave you short?''

He shrugged. ''I always keep some extra on hand. Besides, you can pay me back when you make your regular run.''

''Really?'' She leaned a hip against the truck and cocked her head at him. ''What's in it for you?''

His eyes darkened. ''Well, if you don't have to spend an hour running to the warehouse club, you've suddenly got some time on your hands, now, don't you?''

''I suppose I do,'' she allowed thoughtfully. ''I wonder what I should do with it? I guess I could go over to the library and see if they've gotten in anything new. Or I could go over to the launderette and wash my sheets. I've been going through a lot of sheets lately,'' she said with a wicked grin. ''Or I could—''

Shay snaked out an arm and swept her against him. ''Or you could let me take you upstairs and go down on you until you scream,'' he said softly before his mouth closed over hers.

Time became plastic, irrelevant. The trek back to the bar was a blur. She'd managed quite nicely the whole morning, but suddenly she needed him naked, on her, in her.

Part of her.

They got through the door, barely. Mallory started unbuttoning his shirt with impatient fingers, then gave up and just pulled. There was a light tick that she almost didn't hear over the roaring in her ears.

"Is it safe to be doing this here?" he asked, his hands roving over her.

"The custodian's finished up and gone, no one's due in for hours yet," she said, and then caught her breath at the heat of his hand sliding over her breast. "Besides, the door's locked, and I don't want to take the time to climb the stairs." She slipped her hands inside his open shirt and ran her palms over the hard, bare muscle of his chest and shoulders. "God, you've got a gorgeous body. Does O'Connor's have a gym in back?"

Shay laughed against her mouth. "I bench press kegs during slack times," he said, then pulled her to him. "You're amazing," he murmured. "The first time I saw you dancing, I almost couldn't breathe. It was like I could see what it would be like to make love with you. It made me think about what you'd look like dancing up there naked."

Mallory tugged his shirt loose from his jeans. "And did you do a good job?"

"My imagination was unequal to the task," he said, sliding his hand down over her ass and making her wiggle closer to him. "Reality was beyond anything I could come up with."

Mallory slipped her arms around him and ran them up his bare back, luxuriating in the heat of his body. "So you wanted to see me dancing naked on the bar?" she asked, watching his eyes turn heavy and dark. "Maybe I should see what I can do about that fantasy."

She crossed to the jukebox and punched in a code. A humming bass line began, then the low chords of an organ, then the pulsing beat of Don Henley's "Dirty Laundry" rose around them. Nodding her head to the beat, Mallory moved behind the bar and climbed the steps that led to the top.

Shay watched as she strode onto the wooden surface, long and lean in her jeans, red heels winking. Her hips swayed to the music, with a little snap, a little sashay. She ran her hands down her sides, over the flare of her rear end, then back up to her waist. Drumbeats joined the metronomic organ as she shook her long tumble of sable hair. Her hands flirted with the bottom of her T-shirt, inching it up bit by bit to show the smooth, flat expanse of her belly.

Shay reached a hand behind him to locate a chair and settled into it, staring at the teasing expression on her mouth, the promise in her eyes as she danced for him and him alone. The first time he'd watched her dance, he'd thought that she looked like a woman dancing for her lover.

Now she was.

Mallory whipped off the shirt, tossing it on a table, and his pulse speeded up. Her hands slid up over her breasts, teasing the nipples through the satiny fabric of her bra until he could see them harden into buttons. Turning her back to him, she swayed to the music, wrapping her arms around herself. When she spun back around, her bra was unclasped and her breasts stood out firm and full.

And his mouth went dry.

This time, when she tossed the item of clothing, she aimed toward him and it landed in his lap, soft and silky and black as midnight sin. It smelled of her.

The song was growing more intense, the singer wailing, and Mallory moved up and down the bar as though it were a runway, now crouching down with her hands planted between her knees to press her breasts together, now standing up and moving rhythmically, running her fingers back through her hair. When she unbuttoned her jeans and teasingly pulled down the zipper, he found himself rising to his feet without volition. Then she turned her back to him and slid them down slowly, far enough to show the black thong that she wore, then down to the tops of her thighs. The tiny triangle of black lace made him immensely aware of the smooth roundness that framed it. Heart-shaped, he thought driftingly. Her ass was the shape of a perfect heart.

Shay moved toward the bar as though caught in a spell, watching as she turned to face him again, the lace front of the thong making a vee between her legs. He settled down on a bar stool at her feet, staring up at her as she swayed to the music, cradling her breasts in her hands.

Her thighs were lithe and lovely and she sank down into a crouch directly in front of him, then sat on the bar, her eyes hot and filled with promise.

Her leg stretched out beside him at eye level, the hot red stiletto gleaming. When she stretched out the other, Shay slid off her shoes and let them drop to the floor.

Mallory leaned back on her elbows and watched as Shay pulled at the cuffs of her jeans, stripping them off of her with exquisite slowness. His palms were warm against her skin as he circled her ankles with thumb and forefinger, then slid his hands up her calves. She shivered as she felt the warmth rising, to her knees, to her thighs. Anticipation jittered through her as she watched him lean in and felt the heat of his breath.

Shay hooked his fingers in the sides of her thong and slowly pulled it down over her thighs, her calves, and off her feet, leaving a trail of sensitized skin in its wake. For a moment, he simply looked at her while desire thrummed through her until she quaked. The wanting made her weak, the waiting made her rigid with impatience. Then he leaned in toward her, draping her legs over his shoulders.

His breath was hot against her as he ran his tongue up the tender insides of her thighs, kissing the fragile skin at their apex. The tip of his tongue teased the folds of flesh, and she groaned in frustration. She craved his mouth against her. Instead he tantalized her with the lightest of touches, tormenting her with desire. Unable to help herself, she shifted and made a little moan of protest.

The sound turned into a cry as he pressed his mouth against her, hot and wet and relentless. She arched into mindless orgasm, tossed over the first peak, shuddering against him.

Once she'd stopped quaking from the aftershocks, she opened her eyes and started to lift one leg over his head.

''Huh-uh.'' Shay held it in place and began running his hands over her stomach and up to her breasts. ''Until you're screaming, I think I said. I'm not finished by a long shot.''

Mallory gave a sharp cry as his tongue slid against her. She let her head fall back and closed her eyes, focusing on the sensation. She felt his fingers squeezing her nipples, sending little shocks racing through her as he traced tormenting patterns against her most sensitive places. She arched in shock, gasping as he scraped his teeth over her clitoris, then sucked until every part of her, every muscle, every nerve, every thought tightened down to that one spot. Tension spread through her, unbearable, all of it focused on the point where his mouth touched her, dragging her closer to the edge, and closer still.

Until she tumbled over, gasping and crying out, shuddering again and again. It went on a long time; the aftershocks lasted even longer. Finally she was still, languid and sated.

Shay's face was strained when she sat up and climbed down to the floor. Mallory leaned up against him, her breath still uneven. "I think you need to catch up a little," she whispered, unzipping his fly and pulling out his hard, heavy cock.

Shay spun her around and bent her over. Surprised, she groped for the edge of the bar to steady herself. Then he slid into her in a surge that had her crying out. The strokes were fast, hard, and deep, racking her body with shivers, tearing moans from her. It was quick, savage, and she gloried in it. She felt him grow thicker, harder with each movement. He leaned forward to fill his hands with her breasts, managing one stroke, two, three. Then he groaned and spilled himself in her, pulling her hips hard against him, their moans mingling.

"THREE HARP, ONE BUSHMILL'S, Col," Fiona said, setting her tray on the bar.

Colin stuck a glass under the tap. "It is beyond dead in here. I'm glad I'm out of here soon."

"Things will liven up later, you can be sure. It's

Friday. Of course, I won't know because I'll actually be out for once. Almost like a normal person, then.''

"You've got plans?'' he asked in surprise. "I was figuring you and Shana and I could hit the movies.''

"And listen to you mutter about the subtitles? No, thank you.''

"You and your subtitles. You know there's a reason they invented talking pictures. If I want to read, I'll get a book.''

"It's that Irish love of poetry, me lad,'' she said with a sassy wink. "Anyway, you should like them as well. After all, song lyrics aren't so very far from poetry, some of them. And didn't I notice my Yeats book moved last time you took a break?''

He started filling another pint, then reached behind him to get a glass for the whiskey. "Guilty as charged. Who knew you were so sharp eyed? Anyway, I'm just trying to improve myself.''

She studied him from under her lashes. "Ooh, it's a tall order, that.''

"So where are you and Shana going tonight?'' he asked, pouring whiskey into the glass.

"Oh, we thought we'd look in on Bad Reputation.''

"You what?'' He did a double take. "What are you doing going to a place like that? It's a guys' place. There's nothing there for you. You're wasting your time.''

Fiona gave Colin a sharp look as she took the whiskey from him. "Well it's my time to waste, then, isn't it?''

"It's tacky.'' Colin glowered at her and put a final pint glass under the tap.

"You're just threatened by a bunch of women who aren't afraid to enjoy their sexuality.''

"Hey, I'm all for enjoying sexuality. If it's a strip bar, call it that and get it out of Washington Square. If you're going to be right in the heart of the waterfront, though, keep it clean. This isn't Bourbon Street in New Orleans. I mean, it's not trying to be a strip bar, I'll give them that, but it's everything but."

"And how would you be knowing that, Mr. Arbiter Of Western Taste?" Fiona challenged him.

"I've just been hearing things." A slow tide of red began creeping up his cheeks.

"Oh, and it's a surprise you haven't taken a look yourself."

"Take a look at what?" Colin's sister Shana leaned against the bar. "Two pints of Murphy's while you're at it, Col."

"The depraved dancing girls at Bad Reputation, that's who," Fiona answered her. "He thinks they're going to ruin the morals of everyone in Newport."

Shana laughed, tucking a strand of hair behind her triple-pierced ear. "As if. Colin, you old fuddy-duddy. He likes to think he's much more free-thinking than our stodgy Shay, but he's really no better," she confided to Fiona.

"So I've already told him," Fiona agreed.

"Hey, I'm here, in case you haven't noticed," Colin said, setting the last glass on her tray. "I'm just saying that if you guys are going out tonight, you might want to skip that bar. I mean, it's too loud to talk and the only thing to look at is the dancing girls."

"Well, maybe we like looking at dancing girls, did you ever think of that?" Fiona challenged him, eyes sparking with devilry.

"Yeah." Shana threw Fiona a wink and slung an

arm around her waist. "How do you know what we get up to?"

Colin gave them a thoughtful look. "If you weren't my sisters, I'd ask if I could watch."

"I'm not your sister, Colin O'Connor," Fiona flared.

"I was joking, Fee," he protested. "When did you get such a thin skin, anyway? A person would—" He looked beyond them and his eyes grew round.

Fiona and Shana turned to follow his stare and saw Shay walk through the door with a willowy, dark-haired woman.

"Good Lord," Fiona began, "isn't she the one who was in here the other day?"

"Who's she?" Shana asked suspiciously, studying the woman with her big brother.

"I think she runs Bad Reputation," Colin answered.

THREE PAIRS OF EYES WATCHED Shay avidly as he walked up to the bar. Though part of him itched to touch Mallory, he figured he'd been right to stay hands off for now. No reason to give the happy trio anything more to talk about than they had already.

"About time you showed up," Colin said to Shay, looking speculatively at Mallory. "Your shift starts in half an hour. You're practically late. What have you been up to?"

"Oh, this and that," Shay said blandly, watching Mallory, who was suddenly very absorbed in her fingernails. "This is Mallory Carson. She runs Bad Reputation. Mal, this is my sister Shana and my honorary sister Fiona. And this guy here is my brother Colin."

"Nice to meet you," Mallory said, shaking hands

all around. "Do you ever hire anyone who's not an O'Connor?"

"We have a few imports. Fiona's from Galway."

"Really?" Mallory asked. "I've always wanted to see Ireland. Do you miss it?"

"Now and then," Fiona admitted. "They've more men with good sense over here, though, present company excepted," she said with a sniff at Colin.

"I see," Mallory said, fighting a smile. She glanced at Colin, then she turned to look at him more carefully. "You look really familiar," she said slowly. "Weren't you in Bad Reputation the other night?"

Two feminine heads snapped around to stare at him.

"Oh was he?" asked Fiona.

"I might have dropped in to take a look," Colin muttered, turning around to grab a glass.

"You won the tequila shot contest, didn't you?" Mallory's smile suggested she understood the lay of the land.

Colin looked uncomfortable. "I just had a drink."

"Or three. Belinda was quite taken with you," she said lightly.

"Consorting with immoral bar dancers, are you?" Fiona jibed, picking up her tray. "Now whose morals are in danger?" She flounced away, leaving Colin looking sheepish.

"Are napkins all you need, Mallory?" Shay asked, ducking behind the bar. "Give me a minute and I'll go get them."

"I'll help," Colin volunteered suddenly. "Shana, can you hold the bar for a sec?"

"Make it quick. I've got to get back to my tables."

Shay walked through the door to the back room. With another glance at Mallory, Colin followed.

"Man oh man, now that is a woman," Colin said reverently as they walked through the back room.

"Eyes off," Shay said shortly.

"Hey, it's a free country." At Shay's baleful look, Colin subsided. "So are you keeping the competition in business now?"

"They're not our competition and you know it."

"Even so, what are you doing hanging around there?"

"Not entering tequila drinking contests, if that's what you mean," Shay said pointedly.

Colin flushed. "That was one time, and it got me a kiss from that bodacious blonde. But how did you hook up with this one? I mean, she's a babe, but she doesn't seem like your type."

"She's the sister of a good friend of mine. He asked me to look in on her and help her out." Shay walked into the supplies room.

"Your buddy's sister?"

Shay grunted as he reached for a bale of napkins encased in shrink wrap. "Yeah, why?" He handed the package to Colin and reached for another.

"Your shirt's missing a button that you had earlier this afternoon, big brother." Colin gave him a cheeky look. "So, does your buddy know you're playing hide the shillelagh with his sister?"

The twist of anger was sudden and surprising. Shay turned around slowly. "Has it really been that long since I've given you a pounding?"

Colin's grin widened. "You're ready to defend her honor? Man, this is better than I thought."

"Don't push your luck, Col." Shay's words were icy.

Colin gave him a closer look. "I don't believe it,"

he said slowly. "Mr. Upright has a thing for the bad girl."

"Just for that, you can carry both of them," Shay said, pushing the second bale of napkins in Colin's hands. "If you value your life and that ugly mug of yours, you'll keep your mouth shut."

"You can't hurt me. Mom'll get after you."

"That stopped working when you were twelve." Shay stopped and turned back to Colin, taking one of the bales from him. "Look, she matters, plus she's my good friend's sister. And if you say something stupid to her," he said conversationally, "I will hurt you in ways you never imagined. Mom or no Mom." He turned toward the door.

Only to hear a chorus of female laughter.

"SO THE INSPECTOR STAYED around and asked your bartender out?"

"Belinda has more than a few guys dangling from her hook."

"Good for her," Fiona said from behind the bar where she'd filled in for Shana. "I think it's great what you're doing. Everyone should get a little outrageous once in a while. It's good for the soul."

Mallory looked at her in curiosity. "I thought conservative was the name of the game here."

"Ach, here?" Fiona glanced around. "It's cozy, I'll grant you, but it's so boring here I feel like an old maid. I've more than half a mind to come work for you, if you're hiring. If I have one more man tell me I'm like his sister I'm going to scream."

"Don't let them decide who you are," Mallory returned. "You decide. No matter what you do, it's a pretty safe bet that there's someone out there who's not going to like it, so you might as well please yourself.''

"I like that," Fiona said thoughtfully. "I think I'd like working for you."

Mallory took a sip of the club soda Fiona had set on the bar for her. "Stop by sometime if you want, but not if it's going to get Shay hacked off. I've got enough problems there."

"What kind of problems?" Shana asked, coming back up to the bar with a fresh order. "How'd you and Shay meet, anyway?"

"My brother just decided I needed someone watching over me to see that I behave, so he asked Shay for help."

"Well, that's big brothers for you. Shay's good at keeping things straight and narrow," Shana said.

"Oh, Colin's no better," Fiona returned. "He likes to think he walks on the wild side, but he's just as straitlaced."

"Can't be too conservative or he wouldn't have been hanging around Mallory's bar," Shana returned.

"Maybe he thought it fit with his rock star image," Fiona said.

"Rock star?" Mallory asked. "Is he in a band?"

Shana snorted. "Not just any band. They're destined to be the next great thing, or so he says," she added.

"Really?" Mallory asked, her voice thoughtful. "I'm looking for some live music for Bad Reputation."

"Well why didn't you say so?" Fiona asked. "Colin's group is actually quite good, though I'll swear on a stack of bibles I never said that if you tell him."

"Tell who what?" Colin followed Shay out of the back room, carrying the bale of napkins.

"Mallory's looking for a band for Bad Reputation," Shana said. "You should audition. It could be your big break."

His head snapped toward Mallory. "Seriously?"

Mallory hesitated. "Maybe. I mean, I'd have to audition you. Understand, no guarantees. I've got to find the right band." She gave him a speculative glance. "I'd like to hear you, though."

"Well." Colin paused and watched Shay carry out the first bale and set it by the door. Then the corners of his mouth curved slowly up. "I'll tell you what." He locked eyes with Shana and winked. "We're having a party for my parents' thirty-fifth wedding anniversary next Sunday. My band's going to play. You can come hear us then. I mean, we'll be doing a lot of sixties covers, but you'll be able to hear some of our stuff, too."

"Thanks, but it's a family gig. You're not going to want outsiders there," Mallory said uneasily.

Colin laughed. "Trust me, half the town will be there. Shay can bring you."

"Shay can bring her where?" Shay asked from behind them.

"To Mom and Dad's party."

Mallory was already shaking her head. "I don't think so. Thanks, though."

Shana watched Shay intently, and her expression morphed rapidly from reservation to enthusiasm. "Oh, come to the reception," she urged Mallory. "It'll be a lot more interesting with you there."

Somehow, Mallory had the distinct feeling there

was much more going on than she could see. When in doubt, she thought, stay away. "I need to work."

Shana laughed. "So what? Take the night off. You own the place."

"Yeah," Colin added. "Besides, if you're auditioning a band, you're working anyway, right?"

Time for strategic retreat, Mallory told herself. "I'll think about it," she muttered, and glanced up to find Shay nodding, an odd look on his face.

9

MALLORY STOOD AT THE BAR in Bad Reputation, slicing limes. She knew people who hated bar prep, but she actually found it sort of relaxing. Filling the olive and onion bins, pouring salt, setting out the glassware, it all helped her get in the mood for opening time. Which was all too soon, she thought, glancing at her watch.

"Hiya, Mal." Belinda waltzed in, dressed in skin-tight white hip huggers and a black crop top. Mallory had seen her wear a shirt that was lower cut at some point in time, she figured, but she couldn't remember when.

Belinda disappeared in the back to drop her purse and came back out. "What do you want me to do?"

"Take over the limes. I need to get some popcorn popping for the snack bowls. It's Sunday, which means it'll be football again, and if that gang of guys from last week shows up, we'll need it."

"Oh, the tequila shot crowd?"

Mallory nodded. "The Patriots won and the Jets lost, so someone's going to be buying drinks."

Belinda shook back her blond hair and picked up the knife. "I thought the tall guy was cute. He asked me out, you know."

"And you know the rules," Mallory reminded her, mentally tallying the bottles that needed refilling.

"I know." Belinda pouted. "You have no idea how many dates I've turned down since I started here. I'm going to be an old maid."

Mallory eyed Belinda's fresh, unlined face. "Oh, yeah, I can see you turning into a crone in front of my eyes."

"Hey, it would be nice for a change to have a guy that wasn't always flirting with other women and forgetting his wallet."

"You and Dominic have a fight again?" Belinda's on-again-off-again romance sent the woman through cycles of joy and anguish that often spilled over into work.

"Dominic doesn't deserve me," Belinda snapped bad temperedly. "I'm going to find someone who does."

Mallory stepped through to the door to the back bar and began setting up the popcorn machine. The desperate need people had for steady involvement baffled her—she felt best when she was on her own. It was safer that way. Sure, affairs were nice, sex was great, but getting close to someone was dangerous. You got too close, you stopped being careful. You stopped being careful, you got blindsided.

Or you got pulled into someone else's life, she thought, trying to avoid thinking too much about the O'Connor anniversary party. Though she'd done her best to say no that day in O'Connor's, she had a pretty good idea that no one had listened. The fact that Shay hadn't mentioned it since made her more uneasy than not—knowing him, he was probably assuming that she'd just fall into line.

She didn't belong at a family occasion, especially not one with his family. The fruit didn't fall far from the tree. Shay's staidness likely meant that his family was even more so. An evening celebrating with a group of quiet types? Not her cup of tea, thanks very much.

Mallory walked back in front and rose on her tiptoes to add a bottle of tequila to the liquor wall. A flicker of motion in the mirror had her turning to see Shay.

Mallory put her hands on her hips and gave him a leisurely survey, a smile playing over her lips. "Well, you just keep popping up, don't you?"

"Apparently." His eyes flicked to Belinda, then back to Mallory. "Do you always have your front door open with no bouncer around? If your cash drawer is out, you're taking chances."

"One of my 250-pound bouncers is downstairs filling in the keg room. He'll be up any minute." Mallory heard a little sniff next to her and suppressed a smile. "Excuse me. Shay O'Connor, this is Belinda Nichols."

"Nice to meet you." Belinda shook his hand. "Hey, haven't I seen you in here before?"

"Shay owns O'Connor's, a few blocks over. He comes here every now and again to see how a real bar is run."

Shay shot her a look. "Cute."

Mallory gave him an unrepentant grin. "You're spruced up tonight, Shay. Going somewhere special?"

"Yeah, as a matter of fact. With you."

Mallory blinked. "What's that supposed to mean?"

Behind them, Benny walked in the front door. "Got a group of rowdies coming this way. Are we open?"

"Of course we are, as long as they have ID and money to spend," Mallory said and ducked under the walkthrough to go program the jukebox.

Shay followed her.

"What are you doing here?" she asked testily. "I'm working."

"In case you've forgotten, we have plans tonight."

Just then, a group of loud frat-boy types banged through the door and headed for the bar. "I've got this place to run," Mallory said, nodding toward the bar as the jukebox started playing Kid Rock.

"Don't you have anyone coming in besides Belinda?"

"Liane just walked in and Kayla's due any minute."

"Let's get going, then."

"Shay, I'm not going to your party. When I told Shana I'd think about it, I was just trying to be polite." She punched more buttons on the jukebox, trying to ignore him.

He took her hand, and suddenly ignoring him was no longer an option. "Colin's expecting you to be there to listen to his band. Besides—" his eyes flicked over her "—my parents want to meet you."

Mallory snatched her hand back as though it were burned. "No way."

"Why?" he asked, watching her with interest.

"Look," she said, backing away. "I don't do the family thing. It was sweet of your brother and sister to invite me—"

Shay snorted. "It wasn't sweet. They were trying to yank my chain."

"Then I doubly don't need to be there," she said emphatically.

"Look, all Colin's been talking about for two days straight is having you there to audition the band. He's told the band members, he's told the family, he's told everyone. As far as he's concerned, getting looked at by a real promoter puts them one step from the big time.'' He paused, and she saw the big brother in him then. ''Look, he's young and maybe he got carried away, but in a way, you let him. If you weren't going to come, you should have told him way before now.''

''I want to hear his band,'' she protested, trying to ignore the little wave of guilt. ''I just don't want to do it tonight. Not at a family event, anyway.''

''Why are you so spooked about it? They're just people.''

''Stop trying to push my buttons, Shay,'' she bridled. ''I'm sure it will be a perfectly nice party, but I'm going to pass. Families make me nervous.''

''Why? You have one, don't you? I mean, Dev's normal. Do the rest of yours shoot fire out of their eyes or something?''

''Let's just leave my family out of this, Shay,'' she said, her voice edgy. ''Other people's families bother me, okay? I don't do all the brotherhood and bonding thing.''

''Well, you need to do it tonight. My mother knows I'm seeing you and that you're coming to hear Colin's band.''

''You and I are not seeing each other,'' Mallory hissed, with a quick glance at Benny walking past. ''We're having an affair, that's all.''

''Look, Colin opened his big mouth and she's been all over it for the last two days. I am not going to get any peace until she meets you.''

Horrified, Mallory stared at him. ''Are you out of your mind? Not in a million years! Families are bad enough, but going to a party to be trotted out for your whole clan and dissected as not good enough for your mother's precious boy? Not no, but hell no.''

''How do you know she's going to think you're not good enough? She might love you.''

Mallory gave a humorless laugh. ''Trust me, I've been there before.''

''Am I going to have to pick you up and carry you?'' he asked impatiently. ''Look, all I'm asking you to do is show up, listen to Colin's band and make nice for an hour.''

She put her hands on her hips. ''And I should do this why?''

His gaze flicked toward the ceiling. ''Because I'm asking you as a favor,'' he said simply.

Finding out she had a soft side where he was concerned came as a surprise. And although ''no'' was on the tip of her tongue, she found she couldn't quite say it, no matter how much she dreaded the alternative.

''I can't leave the place without supervision,'' she said, trying for an honorable out.

''Who ran the place last Tuesday?''

She hesitated while he watched. ''Belinda,'' she said finally, with reluctance.

''Well, there you go. She's obviously capable. Take a night off, why don't you? Who knows, you might even have fun. Besides, like Colin said, it's still work as long as you're auditioning the band.''

''I'm responsible for this place. What if something happens while I'm gone?''

''Do you have insurance?''

''Of course.''

''Then come on.''

She hesitated and looked to where Kayla was dancing on the bar for the frat boys. ''I can't go over there like this, Shay. I'm dressed for work, not a family party,'' she protested, with the sense of a losing battle.

He glanced at his watch. ''We've got time for you to change, if you're quick,'' he said, looking down at her red miniskirt and tight white top.

She started to turn toward the door, then stopped and raised her chin. ''No,'' she bluffed, ''I'd rather go like this.'' Given a choice between taking her to meet the parents all tarted up or making her excuses, she was sure he'd choose the latter.

He didn't. ''If that's what it takes to get you there, then come on.'' He stood back and looked at her. ''You'll wake people up,'' he decided, and took her hand.

''HOW DID I LET YOU TALK ME into this?'' Mallory muttered as they neared O'Connor's. ''I hate family things.''

''So you keep saying. You'll like these folks.''

''Easy for you to say. You're probably related to them all.'' Her stomach roiled. If she'd just changed when she'd had a chance, at least she wouldn't stick out like a sore thumb.

Shay opened the door for her and she paused for a deep breath. Then she felt the heat of his palm in the small of her back. *No apologies,* she reminded herself. *Be who you are and forget 'em if they can't take a joke.* She lifted her chin, smiled, and walked through the door.

The warm, crowded space buzzed with noise and energy. Linen tablecloths and flowers dressed up the tables. Garland swooped from the dark wooden beams of the ceiling. O'Connor's had always been a place of cozy comfort. Now, it was filled with noise, laughter and what looked like half of the people in Newport.

She leaned toward Shay. "Don't you need to work?"

He shook his head, hanging her leather jacket on a hook. "We hired caterers. My only job is to relax and show you around."

"I thought I was here to audition Colin's band and split," she said uneasily. As far as she was concerned, the sooner that happened, the better.

"In good time, all in good time." Shay pulled a couple of fluted glasses of champagne off the tray of a passing waiter and handed her one.

Mallory took a sip and felt the bubbles break against her teeth. "Who are all these people, anyway?"

"Family, friends, neighbors. My family's been in business in this town for a lot of years. After a while the contacts start becoming friends."

"Scary thought," she said.

He tipped his head and studied her. "Why would you say that?"

The more relationships you had with people, the more people you had who wanted things from you, she thought, but it seemed churlish to say in the face of all this bonhomie. "Just think of their Christmas list."

"I suppose," he said, but his face said he didn't believe her.

"So you've got about half the population of Newport here," Mallory said, feeling the glow of the champagne start to spread through her.

"Maybe a quarter."

"Better hope the fire marshal doesn't stop in."

Shay fought a smile. "Oh, he's over there in the corner talking to my uncle Sean."

The fire marshal glanced up to see Shay pointing to him and waved.

"Guess it pays to be well connected," Mallory said sardonically.

"Family and friends matter, I think. Don't you?"

She chose not to answer. "So let's get this over with. Who's who?"

"Well, the guests of honor are at the table with all the flowers. My mom's the one in the blue and my dad's the one whispering in her ear."

Mallory looked across the room to see a woman in a flowing periwinkle dress laugh and throw her arms around the rakish-looking man at her side. It was easy to see where Shay and his siblings had gotten their looks, she mused. "How long did you say they'd been married?" she asked, watching Shay's father plant a frankly salacious kiss on his wife.

"Thirty-five years today." His voice held equal parts fondness and pride. How strange, she thought, to look across a room and see parents who were a unit, who always had been. What would it have been like to grow up with that? Was it any wonder he could think of family without flinching?

Was it any wonder she couldn't?

She felt a tap on her shoulder. "Where have you gone off to?" She turned to see Shay watching her intently.

"Nowhere." She waved her hand vaguely. "Just thinking. So who are the rest of the people?"

"Well, you've seen my uncle. The spry old guy in the corner is my Grandda Padraic. He inherited O'Connor's from his father."

"*The* O'Connor?"

"Indeed. He worked at an ale house and scraped up enough money to buy it from the owner when he retired. And the rest, as they say, is history."

Mallory studied the diminutive old gentleman in the bow tie and hunter plaid jacket. "Did it cause bad blood that your father chose to do something else?"

"Not so much as you'd expect," Shay said easily. "They're proud to have a lawyer in the family, and anyway, there was me to take over the business." He plucked a spiral of puff pastry wrapped around olive tapenade from a passing tray and handed it to her.

"You had to start it so young, though." She took a bite of the hors d'oeuvre and almost swooned at the flavor.

"Lots of kids have jobs at seventeen and eighteen," Shay observed, watching her single-minded enjoyment of the food. She'd relaxed in the past half hour, he thought, though he doubted she noticed. The edginess that had stood out all over her when they'd walked in had smoothed away, no doubt helped by the champagne.

"They don't take responsibility for entire businesses," she argued. "Couldn't one of your dad's siblings have taken it over?"

"No other sons to pass it to," he said simply.

She raised a brow. "And daughters weren't good enough?"

"Grandda wanted it to be in the O'Connor name. Besides, he was raised to be big on the eldest son inheriting."

"Chauvinist," she sniffed.

Shay smiled. "You're talking about a man born in 1922."

"Sounds like he stayed there."

Shay turned his head across the room. "Well, you can tell him that yourself, because here he comes."

Mallory watched Shay's grandfather make his way across the room, leaning jauntily on his silver-topped cane.

"Hello, young Shay. Good to see you've finally joined us. You've had your mother worried."

Shay put a hand on Mallory's back and urged her forward. "I had to find my date. Mallory Carson meet my grandfather, Padraic O'Connor. Grandda, meet Mallory. She runs a bar on Washington Square."

"Woman running a bar?" he asked, looking up at her suspiciously. "What do you do if a fight breaks out? You need to be able to break it up."

Given that he was a head shorter than she was, Mallory doubted he was much more effective at stopping brawls than she was. "I have a couple of hired bruisers to keep the clientele in line."

"Good," he nodded vigorously. "You'll need it to stop trouble, especially dressed half naked as you are."

"Padraic O'Connor, you old coot, stop diviling the girl," said a woman's voice behind them. Mallory turned to see a silver-haired woman about Padraic's size behind them. "She's a friend of Shay's and a guest. Remember your manners," she said sharply.

"Ah, Mallory, meet my great-auntie Lillian, Grandda's sister."

Mallory found her hand taken in a surprisingly strong grip. "It's nice to meet you, dear. You'll have to forgive Padraic. We tried to raise him right but it didn't take, and he's just gotten worse with age." She shuffled a step closer to her brother. "The way she's dressed is the style these days. If you ever opened a magazine or newspaper, you'd know that. Join us in the twenty-first century, will you?''

''At my age, I don't have to do anything I don't want to,'' he retorted, a mutinous look on his face.

''With you, that's been any age,'' she retorted.

''Let's just leave them to it,'' Shay whispered, drawing her away. ''They entertain each other for hours this way.''

Mallory followed him bemusedly. ''How much older is she?''

''Six years. She practically raised him, to hear her tell it. He says he'd sooner have been raised by wolves.''

''I can imagine,'' she said, a smile quirking her lips and she watched the bickering pair.

Shay rested a hand on the small of her back. He had a way of touching her like that, lightly, casually, so that it never felt suffocating. It didn't feel like something he was doing before making a pass. It felt…friendly, she realized with surprise. Companionable. It had stolen over her the same way as his small courtesies.

''Let's go meet the guests of honor,'' he said, steering her through the crowd.

Her stomach tightened a little as Shay's mother caught sight of them. Here it came, Mallory thought. Here was where the evening got unpleasant. The quick look up and down, the little hesitation before she came toward them, Mallory had seen it all before.

What she hadn't seen, though, was a mother who stretched out both arms and took her hands in a warm grip. ''You must be the Mallory that Colin's been going on about. You're as beautiful as he let on,'' she said, nodding to herself. "I'm Gillian, Shay's mother. It's so nice to meet you." She released Mallory's hands. "I've heard so much about you from Shana and Colin. I can't get Shay here to tell me a thing."

Her husband was behind her, his hand held out. "Aidan O'Connor," he said. "Good to meet you."

Mallory shook his hand in bemusement. Impeccable manners for both of them, she thought. She figured they had to be nonplussed, at the very least, but they were doing a good job of covering it up.

"Gilly, we should go say hello to Miss Hanover before she goes home. You can grill the girl later," Aidan said, patting Mallory's shoulder.

They drifted off with smiles, leaving her pleasantly puzzled. She'd been prepared for icy politeness if not the cold shoulder. Instead they'd treated her like she was anybody else. Perhaps it was genuine.

Or perhaps Shay's mother was merely biding her time.

Shay handed her another glass of champagne. "To running the gauntlet," she said, raising her glass to his.

"Oh, come on, they were fine."

"They were nice," she confessed. "I was surprised."

"I don't know why. What did you expect?"

Mallory shrugged. "Disapproval, I suppose."

He laughed. "They've got five of us running around getting in trouble. There's not a whole lot that alarms them anymore."

"So there's you, Colin, and Shana. Where are the rest of them?" she asked.

"My brother Ian is a firefighter out in Pittsburgh.

Megan is over doing her year abroad at Dublin University. She wants to be a biochemist.''

''And Colin wants to be a rock star.''

''This week.''

''What about Shana?''

''Shana wants to be a kept woman and never work another day in her life,'' said the woman in question as she walked up. ''Don't look so shocked, Shay, it's a perfectly fine career move. Look at that Hollywood madam who made all the headlines.''

''You're out of your mind, you know,'' Shay told her.

Shana turned to Mallory. ''You've monopolized her long enough, Shay, it's our turn.'' Shana gave Mallory's arm a tug. ''Come on over and talk with Fiona and me. You can meet the cousins.''

Mallory gave a desperate glance to Shay before letting herself be walked away. ''I'll never keep all these people straight.''

Shana waved it away. ''You don't have to. We don't stand much on ceremony. 'Hey you,' usually works.''

Mallory laughed. ''I suppose you know you've completely scandalized your brother.''

''I wouldn't say stuff like that if it weren't so easy to get him in an uproar,'' Shana confided with a laugh. ''I'm loving watching him around you. He has no idea what to do with you and he can't stay away.'' She clicked her glass against Mallory's. ''Here's to you for giving my brother someone to worry about besides Colin and me.''

THE TIME DRIFTED BY in a confusion of stories and laughter, names and faces she'd never remember. Always, Shay was there, either at her elbow or warming her with a glance across the room. When the music started, she danced with uncles, Shay's father, the fire marshal and the head of the Chamber of Commerce. And much to her surprise, she found herself having fun.

She opened the door to the ladies' room, only to find Shay's mother, Gillian, in front of the mirror. No point in pretending she opened the wrong door, she thought. Might just as well get it over with.

"Well hello again," Gillian said, fluffing her hair. "Having fun?"

"Of course. Congratulations. Thirty-five years of marriage is something to be proud of."

"It is, isn't it?" Gillian smiled. "Does it count against me that I've wanted to murder him in his sleep on more than one occasion?"

In spite of herself, Mallory laughed. "No, I'd say it would count against you if you'd managed to live with someone all that time and *not* want to murder him in his sleep."

"That's a relief," Gillian said and leaned against the sink to look at Mallory appraisingly. "So you're the one with the dancing girls."

She'd known this part was coming sooner or later, Mallory thought and raised her chin. "People need entertainment. We just give them what they want."

"I miss letting off steam like that," Gillian said wistfully.

At Mallory's startled glance, Gillian laughed. "I might be fifty-eight but I'm not a fossil. You didn't invent wildness, you know."

For the life of her, Mallory couldn't think of a thing to say.

Gillian smiled. "Nineteen sixty-eight, boy, that was a time. I was a go-go dancer when I met Shay's father, you know."

Mallory's jaw dropped. "You were a…"

"A go-go dancer in a wire cage," Gillian finished for her. "Complete with white patent-leather boots. It was at a club up in Providence. We watched Goldie Hawn every week on *Laugh-In* and tried to rip off her moves."

"But…" Mallory looked around the staid surroundings. "I don't see how…"

"How I wound up somewhere like this?"

"Isn't your husband a family lawyer?" Mallory asked faintly.

Gillian took a lipstick from her purse. "It's that terminally conservative O'Connor blood. Aidan was a student and needed some shaking up. Those O'Connors all need some shaking up," she confided.

Mallory watched her redden her lips. "Now I know where Shay gets his wild streak," she murmured.

"The boy's finally showing a wild streak? Good," Gillian said in satisfaction. "I've been worried about him."

Mallory turned to look at her, well and truly befuddled. "Why are you telling me all this?" she asked.

"Shay's different around you," Gillian said simply. "He's always worked too much. I keep wishing that he'd learn to take things less seriously. The other kids have inherited some of that from me, but Shay's a sucker for the O'Connor responsibility gene. He needs to learn how to enjoy his life before it's past him." Her look was wistful. "Maybe you can help him with that."

Mallory tried to absorb the irony of being welcomed

precisely because of, not in spite of, who she was. "Does Shay know what you used to do?"

Gillian smiled. "It's never come up, exactly." She dropped her lipstick back into her purse and snapped it closed. "I need to keep some mystery, you know. Have fun, dear."

She winked and walked out the door.

10

THE WHINE OF A SAW and the rhythmic pounding of hammers on wood echoed into her apartment from Bad Reputation below as Mallory sat working on her accounting program. More rapidly than she'd expected, the stage on which bands would perform was taking shape. First up—Colin's band. She'd briefly considered trying to save some money by making the stage herself, but quickly decided that some projects were best left to professionals, especially when they involved the safety of others. Still, the red entry in the capital expenditures column made her wince a little. It was so much more pleasant to focus on the revenues she'd been bringing in over the previous weeks.

"And how do your numbers look?"

She glanced up to see Shay walking toward her from the open door that led down to Bad Reputation. "Not nearly as good as you do."

"Same goes." He gave her a hello kiss that stretched out into long, decadent moments of pleasure. Finally he pulled away. "So you still want to go to the warehouse club?"

She smiled. "Honestly, Shay, you plan the most romantic outings."

"Just trying to impress you," he said modestly. "Are you about ready to go?"

"In two shakes of a lamb's tail." She shut down

her computer and pulled out her shopping list. "I want to check on the construction before we go," she said.

They went through the door and down the stairs that opened out just inside the front door of Bad Reputation. A discreet door, locked during business hours, protected it from prying eyes and hands. It was a convenient, if somewhat noisy, living space for someone just starting a business, and it was included in the lease. If there were problems when she had a night off, she was around. Eventually, Mallory supposed, she'd want to move, but right now it worked.

They wandered over to the dance floor, where a crew was building the low stage.

"Hey, isn't that one of your bouncers?" Shay asked.

Mallory nodded. "Randy's trying to get a carpentry business off the ground. I figured it wouldn't hurt to give him a try."

Just then, Randy looked up and set his tools aside. "Hey, Mallory."

"Hey. You know Shay O'Connor, right?"

"Sure. So, how does it look so far?" He waved at the framed-out stage, his florid, blunt-featured face eager to please.

"Great," she said truthfully, circling the sturdy, squarely built structure.

"We should be done with it by this afternoon and we'll paint it tomorrow. You said it was okay if we took two days, right?"

"Absolutely. Hey, you didn't have steps in the original estimate, did you?"

He shrugged and blushed. "I just thought it might be easier to use that way."

"How much more does that add to the estimate?" she asked.

"Nothing. It's a first-customer discount."

"A first…" She raised an eyebrow. "Is this really your first job?"

Randy shifted his feet and looked over at his buddy. "Well, yeah. I mean, Bill and I, we've both worked on crews for four or five years. This is the first job on our own, though. Except for a deck we built for Bill's mom. It's tough to break in this town. You were the first one to give us a chance." He hesitated. "I don't suppose you'd write us a recommendation when we're done, would you? If you're happy with it, I mean."

"Absolutely. Maybe Shay can put the word around at the Chamber of Commerce, too, huh, Shay?"

"Consider it done," Shay said, watching her.

Mallory nodded in satisfaction. "Good. Hey, I'm heading out to do a couple of errands. Will you take care of locking up if you leave before I get back, Randy?"

"Sure," Randy nodded.

"Great." Mallory started to turn away, then stopped. "And, Randy? No first-customer discounts. You charge me the right price. Run your business like a pro, okay?"

He gave her a bashful grin. "You got it, boss."

On the highway to the warehouse club, Shay turned in his seat and watched her drive.

"You have something on your mind, sweet pea?"

"You, of course, but that's become chronic."

His voice sent a little wash of pleasure through her. He had a way of looking at her, Mallory thought, a way that made her feel like he was touching her whole body. She might have been wearing a sweater and jeans, but she felt naked.

"So, I hear from Colin that you're giving his band a gig. You specializing in mentoring start-up businesses?"

She smirked. "Hardly."

"I don't know. A first-time carpenter, a band with no gigs…"

"Hey, they do a good job, they want to go somewhere. I respect that."

He cupped her nape with his hand, smoothing the downy hairs back there with his fingertips. "You've also got a soft spot for the scrappers."

"I don't know what you mean," she muttered, a faint flush staining her cheekbones.

"Would you have hired Colin's band if he weren't my brother?"

"Of course," she said promptly. "They play catchy stuff that's sexy to dance to. That's the kind of band I want in Bad Reputation. It's a business decision—if they work out, I can get a lock on them early and won't be fighting to book them."

"I still think you have a soft spot."

"I think you think entirely too much," she countered.

THERE WAS NOTHING MORE exquisite than the feeling of skin on skin, Mallory thought driftingly. The workday had come and gone and they were finally wrapped together in her bed. Even now, after they'd spent hours making love, the smooth heat of his chest against her breasts sent little bolts of sensation shooting through her.

"There's something about this bed," Shay murmured, stroking her slowly. "Every time I get near it, I get this insatiable craving for you."

"Becka was right about it," Mallory said.

"What do you mean? Who's Becka?"

"A friend of mine from Lowell. I needed a bed and she was moving in with her guy, so she gave me hers. She said it's magic, that it brings good luck."

"Should we go to Atlantic City?"

Mallory bounced her fist lightly off his shoulder. "Not that kind of luck. Happiness, I guess. She said when her friend gave the bed to her, her life came together."

He looked intrigued. "Any idea how long that takes?"

"I don't think it comes with a timer or anything. I'll just settle for a good night's sleep at some point." She yawned. "All that dancing gets exhausting."

"How did you ever get into that, anyway?" Shay asked, eying her lazily.

Mallory propped her chin on his chest. "Well, I didn't plan it, if that's what you're asking. It was about three weeks after we opened. One of the lights over the bar went out. There were only a couple of people in the place, so I figured I might as well deal with it." She traced a fingertip over the line of his collar bone. "I was up on the bar changing the bulb and 'Honky Tonk Women' came on the jukebox. I just started moving to it a little, and then a couple of the guys in the place started making noise, so I camped it up. Belinda jumped up with me. It was just kind of a lark."

"But one that kept going."

She laughed. "Hey, all the noise brought in a couple of people. The next night, we had people asking about it."

"Instant traffic."

"Far be it from me to look a gift horse in the mouth."

"And the Bad Girls were born. What's with the bad thing, anyway?"

"It's catchy, it plays on the concept." She tried to shrug it off.

"It's more than that, it's got to do with you. Were you the town bad girl when you were young?"

She pressed kisses on his chest. "I think you should start using your mouth for other things besides talking."

"No, really." He put his fingers under her jaw and turned her face to look at him. "Talk to me."

Mallory sighed in resignation. "You probably know that when Dev and I were little, we lost our mom." She kept her voice light, her expression calm. "We moved in with my dad's sister. Aunt Rue's second favorite thing to tell me was that I was a bad girl."

"What was the first?"

"That I was just like my no-good mother." The words came out before she could stop them. Mallory rolled away from him onto her side and stared out into the dimness of the room, swallowing the sudden bitterness in her mouth. "I decided pretty early on that if she was going to give me the label, I might as well have fun earning it."

"Didn't your father say anything?"

Mallory hesitated a moment, then sat up on the edge of the bed. "You know what? I'm starved. Why don't we go see what's in the kitchen?"

"Don't shut me out," Shay returned. "Let's finish talking about this."

"About what? There's nothing to say." She ignored

the roiling in her stomach. "It's ancient history, over with years ago."

"No it's not. It's here in this room with us right now. It's part of everything you do."

"Spare me the psychoanalysis, Shay." She rose to her feet and crossed to get her robe. "Let's go find some food. I think I have a frozen pizza."

Shay looked at her and his jaw slowly tightened. "Great. First we'll eat and then you'll kiss me good night and put me out on the street again."

"Don't give me that." She slid her arms into the silk robe. "I'm giving you food and sex and zero demand for commitment. You should be in heaven."

Abruptly Shay got out of bed. "Thanks for being so accommodating," he said shortly, crossing the room to jerk his jeans off the dresser.

"Come on, Shay, you're making a big thing out of nothing," she said persuasively, ignoring the uneasiness that twisted in her stomach. "We've got a good thing going. Let's not screw it up by getting mad."

"Why should I be mad?" he bit off, buttoning his shirt. "I'm getting laid and I'm getting fed. Why should it bug me that you shut me out any time we get close to going beyond that?"

She blew out a breath. "I told you, I don't sleep well with someone else in the bed."

"And I'm not talking about beds and sleeping." His sudden fury left her blinking in shock. "I'm talking about keeping me out of your life and your mind. You do it all the time. You're so damned proud of those walls, you never even bother to look around and see how empty it is inside. Why won't you let me in?"

"Where did this come from?" Mallory swallowed

through a suddenly tight throat. "We agreed to have a fling, Shay, remember?"

"Yeah? Well, I've changed my mind. I want more." Frustration vibrated in the tense lines of his body.

It was par for the course with men, she thought, fighting the surge of alarm. This was how it always happened. They said no-strings sex, great, then sooner or later they'd pitch a fit about wanting more. That was her cue to say thanks and see you later, and then they'd be out of her life.

But she didn't want Shay out of her life. Panic rose up to choke her. It felt too good to have him around. It felt right. But there were places inside, dungeons in her mind where she couldn't let him go. Couldn't let anyone go, except Dev, who'd been there when they were built. "What is that supposed to mean? Are you handing me an ultimatum?"

"Call it what you like. I want more than just sex, and if you're not willing to give it, then maybe it's best that we figure that out now."

"You can't walk out now, the orgasms are too good," she said with an attempt at flippancy that failed miserably.

Shay stopped and turned to her. "So I can only go when you want me to? I'm only around when I don't crowd you too much? That's not the way it works, Mal. It's a two-way street."

She reached out and brushed her fingers against his face. "Don't ask me for things I can't give, Shay. There's only so much I can do right now. You matter to me, though." She was horrified to hear her voice tremble.

"Then let me in." His voice was passionate in its quiet intensity.

"I can't," she said. At the sight of his face closing up, she rushed onward, her words tumbling over one another. "It's the way I'm built, Shay. Things have happened."

"None of which you'll tell me, right?" he snapped. "You know, the mystery thing might have sucked me in when I was nineteen or twenty. Now it just frustrates me. I don't understand why you won't even try, because I know you're stronger than that."

"I can't change who I am overnight," she cried out. "And I can't change it to please you."

The silence pressed against them both.

"Then I guess we know where we stand." For a moment, he simply stared at her. Then he took two quick strides and seized her face in his hands. The kiss he pressed on her was a mix of fury, frustration, passion, and regret. Before she could react, he'd pulled away. "Goodbye, Mallory."

11

MALLORY STARED AT HER PALE face in the bathroom mirror, adding concealer to hide the dark circles. The difficulty she had sleeping with anyone in the bed next to her had paled next to the sleepless hours she'd been through the past few nights.

It was alarming how great a vacuum Shay had left behind. It wasn't just the sex—she missed laughing with him, saving up things to tell him, talking shop at the end of the day.

When she tossed and turned at night, she told herself that it didn't matter, she was fine on her own, she didn't need anyone around. She told herself that he'd be back. But the phone hadn't rung, there'd been no knock at the door. Time, she told herself as she tried to brighten up her face with blusher. She'd get used to it in time. It was probably just as well that it had ended when it had, before she'd gotten too used to having him around.

Anyway, it wasn't just thinking about Shay that was keeping her up. For almost as long as she could remember, she'd had problems sleeping—sleepwalking, nightmares that jolted her awake at 3:00 a.m., weeks of staring up at the ceiling at night, every muscle in her body crying out for rest while slumber remained stubbornly elusive. It was part of the reason she never let lovers stay over. Tossing and turning became excruciating when you were afraid of waking the person in bed next to you. Having a witness made the whole thing more personal. People who slept normally inevitably began to pry into areas she didn't want to discuss.

The answering machine clicked in the other room, making her jump. Adrenaline surged through her veins. The temptation to run to pick up the receiver was overwhelming, but she made herself wait. It could be a telemarketer. It could be a business call.

It could be Shay.

Heart thumping, she waited to hear what he had to say.

The machine clicked again. "Mallory? Mal, you there?" Dev's voice crackled out of the speaker. "Pick up the phone."

She hurried out into the living room to grab the receiver. "Hey. What's up?"

"Life sucks," he said briefly. "How about you?"

"I've been better."

"That doesn't sound too promising. Got any plans for the weekend?"

"Just work, why?"

He blew out a breath. "I just had a mother of a fight with Melissa. I need to get the hell out of Dodge before I do something I'll regret. I figured I'd come for a visit. That all right?"

"Of course," she said instantly. It wasn't even a decision when it came to Dev. He was the one person she allowed in her life absolutely and completely, without reservations. The one person who was safe, she thought, Shay rising in her mind unbidden.

"I figure I can check out the bar, hang out with you, check in with Shay."

She hesitated a moment too long. "Sure."

"Don't tell me you're still upset about him."

"Of course not." She kept her words casual. "Shay's fine." Except for the little fact that he wasn't talking to her, not that she cared.

"That's good." The line crackled.

"You're breaking up, Dev."

"Sorry. I'm on my cell, driving back from a job site." The crackling faded away and his voice was clear again. "Look, I'll probably head out from here around three, be up your way by eight or nine. Can you set up breakfast or something with Shay?"

It figured, she thought. "Sure, I'll take care of it. Drive safe and call me when you hit Rhode Island."

Mallory hung up the phone slowly, staring out the window. Great. She'd dial up Shay and he'd think she was calling to throw herself at his feet. Perfect.

By the time she'd dialed his number, she was already agitated. She paced restlessly while it rang.

"O'Connor's."

It made her almost pathetically glad to hear the sound of his voice. Need for him—not for sex but for Shay—rocketed through her. Anything it took, she thought for a sudden, irrational moment, she'd be willing to do whatever it took to make him a part of her life again.

Mallory shook her head as though someone had thrown water on her. Not whatever it took. She knew what that was and it was too much. That wasn't her. She didn't do that kind of thing. She didn't let people in and she didn't crawl.

"Hello?" Shay said again.

She swallowed. "It's Mallory."

"Hello." His voice was neutral.

"I'm calling for business," she said immediately.

"I never imagined anything but." His voice sounded calm yet remote.

That stopped her for a moment. "I, uh…" She paused. "I just got a call from Dev. He's coming up for the weekend and he wants to get together to talk about the bar. Assuming you've got the time."

"If it's Dev, I'll make the time."

And then he disconnected before she could say anything more.

MALLORY AND DEV SAT at an outdoor table at the Black Pearl, a wharf-front restaurant, staring across the railing to the white pillars of masts lining a nearby pier. Tall aluminum space heaters sent blasts of warmth down at them. The breeze that blew across the water held a slight edge of chill, warning of the winter that was to come.

The air stirred Dev's brown hair, tossing bits of it into his eyes. He really was a good-looking man, Mallory thought. He'd gotten their mother's bone structure with their father's lighter coloring, blue-green eyes the color of sea glass and light brown hair that became streaked with blond in the summer.

"Did my nose slide around on my face when I wasn't looking?" he asked in amusement.

Mallory grinned. "No, I was just thinking about how you look like a beach boy. Philadelphia, Boston, Newport, Baltimore…you think you'll ever live somewhere that isn't on the water?" she asked idly, listening to the harsh cries of the gulls.

He mulled it over. "I don't know. I've never really thought about it, but I guess I have always stuck by the water. I like it. I think I'd feel suffocated being landlocked.''

''You look suffocated now.'' Mallory studied the lines on strain on his face. ''What's going on, Dev?''

''Melissa and I got into it.''

''Over the wedding?''

He shrugged. ''That's a given. She's got this dream wedding idea that I try to stay out of as much as possible.''

''Outside of ponying up your share to support it.''

''Yeah, but her parents are covering most of it. Hell, if it were up to me, I'd just go to the honeymoon resort and get hitched down there,'' he said ruefully.

''Why are you doing something you don't want to do?''

''Because it's a two-way street.'' Dev stopped as Mallory looked away quickly. ''What, did I say something?'' he asked, looking closely at her.

Mallory shook her head. ''No. It just sounds like another one of Melissa's justifications to get you to do something she wants.''

''Well right now what she wants is to sell my house and buy a new one.''

''What? But you love that house.''

''She says it's old and rundown.'' She could hear his anger.

''Of course it's old. That's what you like about it. And you're renovating it.''

''Well, she wants a nice, shiny new house in the suburbs.''

''Dev, you love that house. If she doesn't understand that, she doesn't understand you,'' Mallory said intensely. ''What is she thinking?''

"Probably that she wants built-in closets," he said wryly.

"So what. Sometimes you have to wait to get what you want. It's called being a grown-up," Mallory said impatiently. "You guys aren't even married yet."

"Not for three months."

Mallory searched for diplomacy. "Dev, think hard about getting tied to someone who doesn't understand what's important to you. Or doesn't care. I don't know. It would sure as hell send me running the other way."

He thought for a moment. "Sometimes it seems like all she's hung up on is stuff. She's shopping, she's buying, she wants a car, she wants a house. Is this really who I want to live with for the rest of my life?"

"You tell me," Mallory said grimly.

He sighed. "Hell, I don't know. I just don't want to give up on it without trying. There was a time I thought it would work."

"So you always say. And when was the last time that happened?"

Long moments drifted by. "A while ago," he said finally. "Before the wedding and marriage took everything over. I keep wondering whether things will go back to normal once the wedding jazz is out of the way. I mean, she's even going on at me about wanting sex too often."

Mallory raised her eyebrows. "'Wanting sex'? Like it's something she dispenses? Dev, it's supposed to be something you do because you can't keep your hands off each other, not because your girlfriend doles it out like a privilege."

He gave a genuine laugh, the first she'd heard him give since he'd arrived the night before. "I definitely waited too long to come up here. Between Melissa and her therapist, I'd started thinking I was some kind of sex-obsessed fiend.''

"If I were engaged, I'd sure as hell hope my fiancé was a sex-obsessed fiend. Otherwise I'd be looking at a really boring marriage.''

The breeze snapped banners floating from one of the yachts moored in the harbor. "So what happens now?'' Mallory asked soberly.

"I guess I go back and have a serious talk with her. If we can't see eye to eye now, you're right, it's not going to change.''

"Don't let her start talking you in rings again.''

"Don't worry, I won't.'' He folded his arms and rested them on the table. "So that's what's going on with me. How about what's going on with you?''

"What do you mean? Things are fine,'' she said lightly. "The bar's going well, I'm getting a night off here and there, we're making money. I mean, you saw it last night. It was packed.''

"Yeah, I saw it. I'm still not sure about the whole bar girls thing. I'd like to get Shay's take.''

"You can ask him yourself, then,'' she said as casually as she could. "Here he comes.''

Mallory watched Shay walk through the café toward them. God, the man was beautiful, she thought, watching the breeze ruffle his black hair. Even if she didn't have feelings for him, it would be a loss to give up seeing that face, staring into those vivid blue eyes. Not to mention having those strong hands on her. She shivered.

Not, of course, that she had feelings for him, she reminded herself. Involvement just brought you grief; Dev was a demonstration of that.

"Shay." Dev's face brightened as he stood up and seized Shay's hand, slapping him on the shoulder. "How've you been?"

"Good to see you," Shay said in genuine pleasure. Then he turned to her and his face set. "Mallory." He nodded, his gaze fixed on hers.

It was like being poleaxed. She should look away, she knew, but looking into his eyes again felt like coming home. For two days, it had been as though vital parts of her body had simply shut down. Now, her heart was pumping again, her lungs were breathing, her senses were registering the world. Still, she couldn't move.

Dev looked from Mallory to Shay and back again. A moment passed and his eyes narrowed.

Shay seemed to give himself a mental shake and pulled out a chair. "How was your trip up?" he asked, focusing on Dev for the first time.

Dev gave him a long, steady look. "Not nearly as interesting as my visit is proving to be."

LUNCH WAS OVER AND THE waiter was clearing away their plates when they rose from the table and headed out of the café enclosure. Shay watched Mallory walk ahead of him and wondered how it was possible to ache so thoroughly at her absence even in her presence. Her voice on the phone the previous day had sent hope vaulting through him until he understood that she was merely calling on Dev's behalf. Now her casual manner clawed at him. Only the dark circles under her eyes had him wondering if things were really so easy for her after all.

Outside of the café area, Mallory glanced at her watch. "Look, I've got to get back to do some prep work. I'm sure Shay can entertain you, and if not, you've got a key to my place." She leaned in to kiss Dev on the cheek. Her eyes flicked to Shay, then she turned and headed back toward the cobbled street that led to Washington Square.

Shay's instinct was to follow, but Dev turned the other direction and began strolling down the wharf. Watching Mallory walk away without knowing when he'd see her again was the hardest thing Shay had ever done. Still, he caught up with Dev, walking along the low, weathered Colonial-style buildings that lined the center of the wharf.

Ahead lay the blue of the bay. To their right, sightseers laughed and chattered as they boarded a blue and white harbor cruise boat. "Oh, the meat grinder dropped the line and they were out before the first turn…" came a snatch of conversation from the yachty looking couple ahead of them.

"I used to come down here a lot when I lived here," Dev said idly, strolling over the creosote-coated planks. "You know, watch the yachts, imagine how it would feel for your biggest worry to be polishing chrome."

Shay looked at the bobbing boats. "I figure they've all got things to stress over, though, whether it's putting Johnny through Harvard or getting into the country club."

"Yeah, that's what I eventually decided, too. Everyone's got their own set of problems. So how long have you been sleeping with my sister?" Dev asked without preamble.

Shay snapped his head around to look at Dev, cursing himself. He'd known he needed to fess up and he'd put it off. Now, it seemed, it didn't need to be put off anymore. "Mallory told you?"

"Christ, Shay, it doesn't take a genius to figure it out." Dev stopped at the railing at the end of the pier and looked at him accusingly. "Something's been going on. I saw how you two looked at each other. I know she's unhappy right now. I can pretty much put two and two together."

Shay sighed and leaned against the wooden rails, guilt washing over him. "Dev, it wasn't anything I planned."

"It just worked out that way? When I asked you to take care of my sister, I didn't mean *take care* of her."

"No." Shay held his gaze. "But I figure that's between her and me. We make our own decisions." And Mallory's decision had been to let him walk away.

"I don't suppose it occurred to you to just keep your hands off of her, did it?"

"Dammit, Dev! Do you think I just jumped your sister so I could notch my belt? You know me better than that."

"I thought I did. I thought I could trust you to look after her, not to jerk her around."

"What's that supposed to mean?"

"Oh come on, do you think she looks like death warmed over because of the bar?"

"What did she tell you?"

"She didn't tell me anything. She didn't have to. I haven't asked yet, but you'd better believe I will before I leave," he said grimly.

Shay closed his eyes. "Look, Dev, I didn't just hop into bed with your sister, okay? I wanted to, believe me, but I did my best to avoid it."

"Bullshit. The whole reason I asked you to look in

on her was because I trusted you, because I knew you had sisters. You think I don't know what she looks like or how she works guys over? I thought I could depend on you to look after her, not let her tease you into taking her and boffing her brains out.''

Shay grabbed the front of Dev's shirt. ''I don't give a good goddamn if you're her brother, you do not have the right to talk about her like that,'' he snarled, the fingers of his free hand curling into a fist. He registered Dev's smile an instant before he would have thrown the punch, and froze. ''Nice,'' he said, tapping Dev on the shoulder with his still clenched fist.

Dev grinned and straightened his shirt. ''Thanks. It's a good thing you reacted the way you did or I'd have been compelled to kick the crap out of you. Big brother's prerogative. That doesn't mean that I'm still not a little bit pissed you've been sleeping with my sister, but at least I don't have to stomp you.''

''Look, it's not something I'm proud of. But...she got to me,'' he said simply. ''I really want to see this turn into something, except she's got these walls up a mile high and I don't know how to get past them.'' He dragged a hand through his hair in frustration.

''Well, I'll be damned,'' Dev said slowly. ''You really did fall for her.''

''I care about her,'' Shay corrected.

Dev studied him. ''Oh, yeah, you've definitely got the look. You're in love with her.''

Fury flowed through him, then acceptance. Then frustration. ''It doesn't matter how I feel. She's so busy shutting me out that I can't find a way in,'' he said tensely. ''I mean, what is it with her?''

Out on the bay, a pelican dove into the water and emerged with a wriggling fish in its bill. Dev bounced his hand lightly on the wooden rail. "I don't even know where to start, Shay. She didn't have a great time growing up. We weren't raised in a storybook family like yours."

"That much I know from the little she's told me."

"Yeah?" Dev asked in surprise. "Well if she's told you anything, you've gotten a hell of a lot further with her than anyone else has."

"A line here or there doesn't cut it, Dev, not when she tells me to leave every night because she wants to keep it light."

"Well it's obviously not so light for her, you've only got to look at her to know that."

"Past a certain point, it doesn't matter what I know. She's got to admit it to herself and she's got to let me in."

"Is that what this fight's about? Some kind of ultimatum?" Dev shook his head. "I don't know beans about relationships, that much should be obvious, but I do know Mallory. She's got good reasons for being the way she is, Shay. You can't force her, though. She'll tell you when she's ready."

"Will she? Or will she just do her lone wolf thing?"

Dev propped his folded elbows on the railing and eyed Shay. "I never figured you for a quitter."

"Is that my cue to try to throw another punch at you?"

"No, that's me telling you to take another run at her. Don't tell me her saying no is all it took for you to walk away. I seem to remember you telling me that stubbornness is an O'Connor family trait."

Shay nodded.

"Well then do your genes proud," Dev said. He

nodded toward the waterfront. "Now let's go see if we can catch the rest of the Penn State game."

THE JUKEBOX WAS SILENT, the doors were locked, and the patrons were long gone when Mallory led Dev up the inner stairs to her apartment, her shoes dangling from one hand.

"Man, I'd rather be framing up a two story house in a day than trying to do what you do," Dev said as she unlocked the door. "I am beat."

"That's what you get for dancing with Belinda all night." She turned on a lamp and sank down onto the couch with a sigh. "Still think the Bad Girls are a bad idea?"

"Hey, Belinda's a nice woman." Dev dropped into the chair.

"Well, she's crushed out on you completely."

"Hardly. By the end of the night she was telling me about some jerk named Dominic."

Mallory grimaced and lay back against the pillows. "He's her idiot of a boyfriend. About every other week she vows to leave him in the dust, but she keeps going back."

"Maybe she cares about him."

"Yeah, well he doesn't care about her, at least not the way she needs to be cared about."

"You never know what goes on between two people. It must work for Belinda or she wouldn't stay with him. The day it stops working will be the day she walks."

"Thanks for explaining that concept," she said with a roll of her eyes. "Is that how it is with you and Melissa?"

"I haven't figured it out yet. But I'm working on

it.'' He got up and walked toward the kitchen. "You got anything to drink around here?"

"There's beer and soft drinks in the fridge. You can grab me one while you're at it." She massaged her foot. "Anyway, the problem with relationships like Belinda's is that they don't work, and it's people like me that wind up listening to the fallout."

"Which you do, I hear," he said, raising his voice so she could hear him. "Belinda spent a lot of time telling me how you were the best boss she's ever worked for and how understanding you've been when she's gotten upset."

Mallory shifted uncomfortably. "Hey, if that's what I need to do to get her in shape to work, I'll do it. She's a top-notch bartender most of the time."

"She also told me you sent her home one night and worked the whole shift alone." He walked out carrying a couple of cans of cola.

"So I'm a sap. What of it?" She took the drink he proffered and leaned back on the couch to crack it open.

"Nice to see you're not entirely bah humbug when it comes to relationships," he said, wandering over to her shelving unit to turn on the stereo.

"Look, relationships are a pain in the neck. They're a complication and waste of time, which is why I avoid them at all costs."

Dev leaned against the kitchen door and looked at her. "You're so tough," he mocked gently.

"What?" she frowned.

"All this talk about flying solo. If you don't need anyone and you're tough as nails, then how is it you've looked like hell all weekend?"

The sharp stab of betrayal caught her by surprise. "I see you've been talking with Shay again."

"Come on, Mal," he said. "I could see what was going on the minute he walked up at lunch."

"Did he tell you it was over?"

"Just that you were trying like hell to make it that way. My question is why?"

She gave him a derisive look. "You grew up in the same house as me last time I checked. Why do you think?"

"Are you really going to let a couple of screwed-up people determine the course of your whole life?" He stalked back to his chair. "I'd have thought you were smarter than that."

"Hey, I'm not the one who's trying to go back and rewrite Mom and Dad's story," she flung at him.

He looked at her levelly. "I'm going to swallow that because I know you only take cheap shots when you're scared."

"Don't go playing big brother on me, Dev," she said hotly.

"Mal, it's not something I play. For better or worse, it's who I am," he said simply. "You think what happened with Mom and Dad just rolled off my back? I was there for it, too, you know. I'm just trying to live my life on my terms, not theirs."

"By trying to hook up with the worst possible match you can find?"

He gave her a hard look. "I'm trying to go with my gut. And if I do marry Melissa, I'll expect you to respect that."

"Sorry," she muttered.

"Anyway, we were supposed to be talking about

you before you pushed us off the topic. You're very good at that, you know.''

''It's intentional, brother dear. There's nothing to talk about.''

Dev raised an eyebrow. ''If Shay doesn't matter to you, then why does it bother you to talk about him?''

''I thought women were supposed to be the ones who were obsessed with talking about their feelings,'' she snapped, sitting up and thumping her feet on the floor. ''Between you and Shay, I can't catch a break.''

''Mal, he cares about you. And you can dodge it all you want, but you care about him. Make whatever decision you want to about him, but make it an honest one. You owe it to both of you.''

12

THE LILTING STRAINS of pennywhistle and fiddle died away, to be replaced by whoops and applause. The end of another successful music evening at O'Connor's, Shay thought, watching the band take their bows. It hadn't been easy to convince the family that music was the right way to go with O'Connor's, but for going on three years he'd been filling up the tavern on Sunday nights with Irish music, blues, jazz and folk.

Most nights, listening to the bands made him itch to open the music club that he dreamed of, the one that would let him tread closer to the edge, taking advantage of Newport's location to bring in emerging talent touring in Manhattan and Boston.

This night, he idly watched the band members take down their equipment, his mind preoccupied with Mallory. Dev had accused him of quitting, of throwing out ultimatums. Sure, he'd made mistakes. He'd made the assumption that her feelings had to be as strong as his or they didn't count, that she had to be willing to act on his timeline.

Shay put his hands on the edge of the bar and leaned. He'd been wrong and he knew it. Still, what was the hope for their relationship if she didn't try to meet him partway? He didn't even need halfway, Shay thought, shaking his head at himself. He'd settle for having her throw him a bone. But she wasn't even willing to do that.

"What the hell does she think she's up to?" Colin snarled under his breath.

Shay jolted. It was as though his brother was reading his mind. Then he looked up to see the direction of Colin's gaze. At the hostess stand, Fiona laughed with a stocky blonde who looked like he'd chosen his clothes from a trendy ad, her red-gold braid snaking wildly down her back. When Trendy Boy held out a napkin, she paused, then wrote something on it. He made a show of holding it to his heart, then blew her a kiss and walked out the door.

Fiona shook her head wonderingly and laughed again as she tripped toward the bar on light feet.

"Conducting your love life on the job, Fee?" Colin asked with an edge to his voice as she walked up.

Her smile faded and her eyes cooled. "And what business is it of yours, Colin O'Connor?"

"O'Connor's is a tavern, not a date factory. You're here to work."

She turned to Shay. "And do you think I was out of line?"

Shay shrugged. "If you did it every week, maybe, but it isn't a big deal."

"Who is he, anyway?" Colin asked. "He looks like some lame guy who spends more time worrying about his wardrobe than anything else."

"I met him the other night at Bad Reputation. He tracked me down," she said in bemusement, glancing back at the door. "I told him I worked at a pub and he found me."

"I'll bet he did," Colin said grimly.

Her smile vanished. "And since when has my love

life interested you?'' she rounded on him. ''Jealous? Or is it that good girls aren't supposed to date? Is that it? I've a right to be a real person, Colin, and if you can't deal with it that's your problem.'' She picked up her tray and stomped away.

''You really are smooth,'' Shay murmured.

''I can do without the commentary, thanks.''

''So why do you care who she dates?'' Shay asked mildly.

''Because she's too naive to realize that that poser is just hanging around hoping to get laid.'' Colin thumped a glass down on the bar so hard it cracked with a sharp tink.

''Easy on the glassware.'' Shay eyed him. ''You're awfully protective of her.''

''Oh, like you aren't? She's like our sister.''

''So you say, although I don't see you that worried over Shana.''

Colin gave a short laugh. ''Shana can take care of herself. God help the man who gets on the wrong side of her.''

''You know what I think, little brother?'' Shay said casually. ''I think you've got a thing for Fiona.''

''You're out of your mind,'' Colin snarled.

''But I'm not wrong.''

''And since when have you been such an expert on relationships? I don't notice you rolling with joy lately.''

Shay looked crossly at him, aware that he was right. He sat here waiting, hoping that Mallory might come through the door and want him again when he'd demonstrated to her that he expected things to happen on his terms or else. She'd be out of her mind to go along with it. And he'd been totally unfair to suggest it.

Abruptly Shay untied his apron and turned to Colin. "It's nearly midnight. Can you handle the place until closing?"

"What?" Colin blinked at him. "Yeah, sure. Where are you going?"

"It's about time one of us showed some smarts about women."

THE SUNDAY NIGHT CROWD was thinner than it had been in previous weeks. Maybe the chill was keeping people in, Mallory speculated, absently filling a drink order with efficiency.

Making a mental note to check the *Farmer's Almanac,* she filled a drink order with absent efficiency. "So what do you think, is it going to be a mild winter?" she asked the rawboned customer as she handed him his beer.

"I sure hope so. If spring started tomorrow, it wouldn't be too soon for me."

"I'm with you," she smiled. Her smile slipped a notch when she saw Shay walk through the door. All day her mind had been on her conversation with Dev. She'd managed to distract herself somewhat by taking him for breakfast at her favorite greasy spoon just off the waterfront, then taking him around the mansions. Much to her surprise, he'd never seen them. For herself, she found the experience different—now, instead of being a sightseer, she was a local showing off her history, and the history seeped through her.

All too soon, though, she was hugging him goodbye and packing him into his truck to go back to Baltimore. All too soon, she was left to face her thoughts alone.

Honesty, Dev had said. If she was honest, she cared

for Shay. He made her feel good without making her feel smothered. But whether she could give him what he wanted was a whole other question. Was he asking about her past because he cared or because, like a little boy, he wanted to take the back of the clock off and see what was inside? And what happened once he saw, would the clock stop being a fascination? It made her palms sweat to think about opening up to him. You did that, you got wrecked; she'd seen that firsthand.

I'm trying to live my life on my terms, not on theirs, Dev's words echoed in her mind. On her terms. Maybe it was time to start thinking about that. It wasn't like her involvement with Shay was anything really serious, she reasoned. Why let her family history scare her away from a good thing? She could bail at any time, any time at all. It could feel so good…

"Belinda?" she said slowly. "Can you close up? I need to do something."

"I—" Belinda turned away from the customer she was chatting up and caught sight of Shay. "Sure."

Mallory slipped under the walkthrough and walked toward Shay, her eyes unwavering on his. She stopped in front of him. "Hey."

"Hey yourself. Did Dev go home?"

Mallory nodded. "This afternoon. I was glad he could stay for a while. It was good to see him."

"Yeah," Shay said and paused. "Listen, do you need to be down here until close or can you get away? I was hoping we could talk."

She gave him a sharp look, then nodded slowly. "Belinda's taking care of things. Let's go upstairs."

The thumping of their feet on the wooden treads echoed the hammering of her heart. When they stepped into the living room, all she could do was think wildly that she wasn't ready.

As soon as they were inside, she was headed for the kitchen. "Can I get you something to drink?" Something to hold, something to at least keep her hands busy.

Shay caught her arm and drew her to the couch. "No serving. You're off the clock. Sit down and relax."

She sat, but with muscles tense with nerves.

Shay took a breath and turned to her. "I wanted to talk with you about the other night."

Tension strung her tight. "I guess I wanted to talk with you about the same thing."

"Me first," he said simply, reaching out to take her hand. "What I have to say is short and sweet: I had no business handing you an ultimatum the other night. I meant it when I said a relationship is a two-way street, but that means that I don't have the right to determine how things progress any more than you do."

Mallory let out a breath she hadn't been aware of holding. "I wasn't trying to be difficult. I just..."

"I know." He raised her hand to kiss her fingers.

Mallory stirred. "So what does this mean? Do we go back to where we were?"

"That's going backward, don't you think?" he asked softly.

Anxiety tightened her voice. "Look, Shay, I don't do relationships. I never have. Frankly they scare the hell out of me. People start talking to me about opening up, my usual M.O. is to walk away." He started to speak and she raised her hand at him. "Let me finish." She took a deep breath. "My usual M.O. isn't working that well with you. You've gotten under my skin and I don't know what to do about it. You want me to open up? This is about as open as I know how to be right now.'' She swallowed. ''I don't know if it's enough, but it's all I can do.''

''I don't think anyone's keeping score.'' His eyes bored into hers. So blue they were almost black, she thought driftingly. Blue enough to dive into, like the ocean water she loved. And when he leaned in to kiss her, she kept her eyes open until the last minute, watching his.

Her first thought when his lips brushed hers was *oh, this is right*. Her second was *I want more*. Her third was *now*. It was like sucking on an Atomic Fireball— an instant of sweet, then a quick tang, then a roar of heat.

When she would have clutched at him and torn at his clothes, though, he held back. ''Huh-uh,'' he murmured, sliding his hands under her. ''Tonight we take it slow.''

Before she could react, he had scooped her up and was carrying her to the bedroom. She pressed her face against his neck to breathe in his scent. Then he laid her on the feather duvet of her bed.

Mallory watched his face, intense with concentration as he undressed her. When she would have moved to help him, he stayed her hands. ''Relax,'' he whispered. ''Let me do for you.''

The light from the living room shone into the bedroom, throwing Shay's shadow against the wall. She watched his silhouette as he unbuttoned his shirt, sliding the cloth off his shoulders. The shadows threw his features into high relief, making him look like some

Greek god as he unbuckled his belt and stepped out of his jeans.

When he came to her, his hands slid over her, so softly that he barely skimmed the skin. The soft brush awakened all her nerve endings, making her tremble. Warm and tempting, his lips followed his hands, cutting a path of sensation across all areas of her body.

She reached down to find him trembling and hard, but the urgency was curiously absent. Instead all was tender and slow, gentle and measured. When he slid into her, his eyes on hers as she cradled his face, it was less about connecting in body and more in mind. He stroked, she accepted, but both of them were tuned into feeling the other's pleasure. And when they both spiraled up to the pinnacle and dropped off, it was together, and they held tight to share the quaking glory.

Later, after they were near drifting off, Shay stirred and made to rise. "I'm going to head out and let you sleep."

"No." Mallory put her hand on his chest, her eyes huge and dark. "Stay. I want you to stay." She gave a shaky laugh. "Don't get too alarmed if I get up and start wandering around, though. And don't expect to sleep too much, mostly because I won't sleep too much."

He slid his hands down her body. "Who said I was worried about sleep?"

THE ALLEY WAS NARROW and pooled in shadow. Fear clogged her throat. "Mallory, come on." It was her father's voice, calling to her from the shadows. With a hammering heart, she stepped into the narrow mouth and began to walk toward the sound of his voice. She didn't see anyone, though, just the shadowy bulk of trash bins and rubbish, and the darker rectangles of doorways. She tried to cry for him to wait, but the words came out in a whisper.

"Mallory, come on." Again the voice, this time impatient and more distant. She tried to hurry, but the pavement was broken underfoot, with loose stones and cracks. Behind her, she heard a rattle of noise and a snuffling as something stirred in one of the doorways.

Stones clicked and she heard the heavy, dragging tread of feet, felt the vibration of something unimaginably large thudding into the ground as it came after her. Adrenaline vaulted through her. She wanted to scream, but only a faint whimper came out. Faster, if she could just go faster she'd catch up with her daddy and everything would be okay. She broke into a run, bouncing off things she couldn't see, tripping and falling. Pain rocketed through her but the fear was greater and somehow she scrambled to her feet to go on.

In the shadows, it moved inexorably toward her, knocking trash cans out of the way so that the racket almost masked her father's voice. "Mallory, come on." The words were faint now, as though he were a very long way away, perhaps around a corner. Perhaps she'd taken a wrong turn.

She opened her mouth to scream for him, but no sound emerged. She was panting now in fear, unable to run back to her last island of safety, unable to go forward. It was nearer now, she could hear the harsh rattle of its breathing. Her legs were leaden. There had to be a way to escape but she couldn't see, she could no longer hear her father, everything was dark. It was going to get her, she thought in despair. The hairs on the back of her neck prickled as she felt something

brush against her skin and she was bolting forward,
she was screaming, she was—sitting bolt upright in
bed crying out. Hands were on her, as in the dream,
and she fought to escape them until gradually awareness returned. It was Shay, she realized, holding her
while her heart thudded in her chest, while her breath
still came in gasps.

His voice was soothing, his hands gentle. "Shhhh,
it's all right," he said softly, rocking her until she
relaxed enough to lie back down next to him, shivering. "Bad dream?"

As always, it left her feeling fragile, shaky. It was
the reason she never wanted to sleep with another.
"Just a nightmare I have sometimes," she said, but
her voice still held too much anxiety to achieve the
offhand tone she strived for. She lay back down in the
circle of his arms. Sleep was impossible to consider.
Alone, she needed to be alone. She had to ask him to
leave.

The thing that would be unforgivable.

"Tell me about it," Shay said softly, kissing her
hair. Talk to him, Dev had said. Trust him. Disorien-
tation from the dream had her leaning her head on the
pillow as he spooned against her.

The silence stretched out. The warmth of his body,
the comfort of his arms around her softened the edges
of the leftover fear, made her feel secure. The dimness
of the room gathered around her like a warm cloak.
"Talk to me," he whispered.

The seconds ticked by and Shay resisted the urge
to ask her again. She'd either open up to him or she
wouldn't. Trust wasn't something you could order up
on a schedule, he understood that now. Just as he knew
that the words wouldn't be something he could listen

to lightly. They would cost them both. *Talk to me,* he thought silently.

And finally, her voice soft as angels' wings in the night, she did.

"I guess you know from Dev that my mother walked out on us. I was about six. We came home from school and she was just gone. Dev found the note on the kitchen table...I never asked what it said. The weird thing was that my dad acted like nothing had happened. He fed us macaroni and cheese and put us to bed." She sighed and Shay pulled her in tighter against him, pulling the covers up over their spooned bodies.

"I woke up and it was dark and I was really thirsty. Mostly I was scared of the big empty. I kept thinking that it was my fault she'd gone away. She'd yelled at me the day before for leaving my room a mess. Deep down, I just knew that if I'd been a better little girl, she wouldn't have left."

"No," he said softly.

"I know, I know, standard psychology," she hastened to say, "but I was six. What did I know?

"Anyway, I finally crawled out of bed and went down the hall to my parents' room. That's what I'd do when I couldn't sleep. Not to crawl in bed with them, but so my mom would get me a glass of water or something. They always left the door open. Except my daddy's door was closed."

A car drove by in the street outside, sending a wash of light strobing through the darkness of the room.

"I stayed outside his room for a long time. I made noises I thought would wake him up so he'd find me in the hall. Things would be better if he'd open the door and come out, I just knew it. He'd tell me it wasn't my fault, that it would be okay.'' She paused for a long time. Shay pressed a kiss to her temple and waited. Finally she began again.

''He never opened the door, though, and I was so thirsty. I finally got up my nerve to go downstairs. I was scared of the shadows and I was tiptoeing. And then I heard a funny noise, like a dry kind of hacking. I didn't know what it was, and then I got close enough to see the shape on the couch. It was my daddy. And he was crying.''

She began to tremble. ''Nothing in my life had ever scared me like that sound. It was like my whole world went spinning off its axis. Daddies weren't supposed to cry, you know? Daddies were supposed to be solid like the earth. Mommies were supposed to take care of you and daddies were supposed to push you on the swings and whirl you around in the sun and introduce you as my little girl. They weren't supposed to sit in the dark crying.''

Her breath had become unsteady. His heart ached for her, for that little girl. ''It seemed like I sat on the stairs there forever. I didn't know what to do. And then Dev was there, taking my hand. He told me it was going to be all right and took me back up to bed.

''My father was never the same after that day. It was like all the strength had left him with my mother. He started drinking. Dev probably told you, he died in a crane accident down at the docks, but if it hadn't been that, it would have been liver damage. He wasn't a mean drunk, he'd just…go away somewhere in his mind.'' Her voice trailed off and he held her close until she spoke again.

''So now I dream about being in dark alleys with my father running off up ahead and scary things chasing me behind. Textbook Freud.'' She gave a laugh that ended in a choke. ''The stupid thing is that it still scares me silly every time. You know, it wasn't just my mom that left that day. My dad left, too, it's just his body hung around a little longer.'' To her horror, her voice broke and suddenly she was sobbing, curling herself into a ball of misery while Shay murmured soothing sounds in her ear. Gently he turned her in his arms and she was pressed against him, holding on to him as the one solid thing in the tempest.

Time drifted by, measured only by the regular stroke of his hand down her back and the soft kisses he pressed onto her eyes. Time drifted by as she wept for all she had lost, for that little girl on the stairs.

Finally her grief abated and she lay against him, exhausted. Sleep beckoned.

''I never cried over it,'' she murmured drowsily, brushing her fingers along his cheek. ''I hurt and I was afraid, but I never cried.''

Shay tightened his arms around her. ''Sometimes you need to let it out. Maybe now you can get past it.''

''Maybe,'' she yawned.

''For now, my love, just sleep,'' he whispered, and followed her down.

MALLORY WOKE TO FIND THE warm press of Shay's body against her. For a few seconds, she didn't wonder at the feel of his arms around her, just nestled into the safety and comfort.

Then memory flooded back and her eyes snapped open in horror. What had she done, Mallory thought with an internal groan. When she'd told him she'd try, she hadn't intended to tell him everything. Not at first. Not before she knew she could trust him.

Keep yourself for yourself, that was what she knew, what she'd always known. Give too much and you hand over all the power. Keep some back.

Instead she'd shown him her private demons. It had been so easy. He'd been there with warm arms and soft murmurs. He'd made her feel safe. He'd offered her his strength and support and in the darkest hours, she'd taken it. She'd given him everything—her past, her tears, her trust. But it was worse than that.

She'd given him her heart.

13

THE DOOR TO BAD REPUTATION stood propped open with a wedge as the loaders from Mallory's distributor brought in her weekly supply of liquor. Bourbon, tequila, vodka and rum, it passed through the door case by case.

Mallory stood next to the truck, trying to concentrate on checking off the order, and focusing on anything but. Love. The knowledge jittered through her, mixing with anxiety. How had she let herself fall in love and what was she supposed to do now? Unable to face Shay that morning, she'd slipped out while he was still sleeping and walked for hours in the early dawn until she knew he was due at O'Connor's and it was safe to come back.

She'd known that he'd become important to her, but she'd thought it was something under her control. She'd thought opening up would let their relationship continue. She hadn't imagined it would result in her giving him everything.

What now, that was the $64,000 question. Breaking things off would be the safest thing. It wouldn't come without a price, though, she knew that much already. Going forward was fraught with risk. Telling him how she felt was out of the question. But could she trust him enough to continue seeing him, knowing that at some point he might guess?

"What about the kegs?" Mallory blinked to find a burly man in a sweatshirt standing in front of her, resting a case of gin on his hips.

"The cold room's in the cellar. Bring the truck into the alley. We've got an elevator in the back to take them down to cellar level."

She glanced up at the pedestrian approaching her and blinked. "Hi, Fiona. What brings you around here?" she asked, taking a final look at the list on her clipboard as the loaders closed up the truck and prepared to drive around to the back.

Fiona hesitated. "Could I talk with you for a minute?"

"Sure." She took a closer look, noting the pale face and dark eyes. "Come on in."

Inside Bad Reputation, it could have as easily been ten or eleven at night as ten in the morning. Without windows, time was irrelevant. Mallory headed behind the bar and pulled out a couple of glasses. "You want something to drink?"

"A soft drink, if you have it," Fiona said, sliding onto a bar stool.

Mallory set out Fiona's drink and poured herself a club soda. She added a quick dash of lime juice and took a sip. "So what's on your mind?" she asked, setting it on the counter.

"I want a job," Fiona blurted.

Mallory studied the girl's face, noticing the lines of strain. "What's wrong with O'Connor's? You've been there since you came over from Ireland, haven't you?"

Fiona tapped her fingers restlessly. "Three years," she said flatly.

"So?"

"Three years of being treated like a bit of wallpaper.'' The torrent of words was sudden, brusque. ''I'm tired of being told who I am. 'Fee, you're a good girl,' 'That's our lass, Fee.' I want to be treated like an adult, not like a storybook character.''

Mallory gave her a shrewd look. ''This wouldn't, by any chance, have to do with Colin, would it?''

''So what if it does? 'She's my sister,' 'She's a good lass,' 'That's our little Fee.' Well, he won't take his chance, will he? And then he turns rude when someone else makes me feel like I'm pretty.''

''Maybe he doesn't know his own mind.''

''Well he should,'' she said hotly. ''And then what does he do but have a fit because a man I've met comes to ask me for a date. It's the most romantic thing that's happened to me, and all Col can say is mean things.''

''Fiona, he's jealous, can't you see that?''

''Well he's got no right to it, does he?'' she flared. ''He's had all the chances in the world and he treats me like I'm invisible. Well, if I'm invisible, then I'll just take myself away somewhere I'm appreciated.''

''Are you sure you're really ready for what it's like to work here?'' Mallory asked gently. ''I mean, there's no hiding. You're going to have guys flirting with you, making passes, trying to get away with the odd pinch or pat if they think the bouncer's not watching. It might look like fun, but you can feel pretty damned naked when you're up on that bar and they're all looking at you like you're on a plate.''

''I think it'll be lovely, altogether. It'll make me feel like a woman for a change.''

Mallory gave her a sober look. ''No man alive can make you feel like a woman. That's something you have to find in yourself.''

"I know," Fiona said. "It's just that the man makes me half mad."

Mallory shook her head in sympathy. "It's a bad sign, Fiona. It's the ones you care about that make you crazy. The ones that don't matter don't bother you at all."

"Well it's high time for me to be getting over Mr. Colin O'Connor and onto other men."

"Don't expect it to happen here," Mallory said mildly. "My one cardinal rule is no dating customers."

A spark of mischief glimmered in Fiona's gray eyes. "I guess I'll have to work quick, then, and catch them before they buy a drink."

Mallory took another sip of her club soda. "I still don't know about this, though," she said, her voice troubled. "Normally I'd say more power to you but Shay will have my head if I steal you away."

"You're not stealing me," Fiona countered. "I'm an adult and I know my own mind."

Mallory gave her a long look. "I want you to think about it for a day or two. Be really sure you want to make the change. If you're still certain, you can try it out once while you're still working for Shay, make sure you like it."

"I'm off Friday night," Fiona said.

"Okay, I'll see you here Friday at eight. Don't be late."

"All right." Fiona turned to go, then stopped partway to the door. "How shall I dress?"

Mallory gave her a wicked grin. "Like a bad girl, of course."

THE WHOLE THING GAVE HER an uneasy feeling, Mallory thought as she did bar prep later that afternoon.

She could tell herself all she wanted that Fiona was an adult and entitled to her choices. Reality was, she still felt like she was stealing one of Shay's staff, a person who was obviously the next best thing to a family member. Worse, she was luring her into a den of iniquity. Not that she'd done any luring—quite the opposite. But she couldn't shake the idea that Shay would not be thrilled. And with things up in the air between them, she wasn't at all sure that adding one more thing to the mix was a wise idea.

The door opened and Mallory realized with a start that she'd forgotten to lock it after the delivery. She sighed and prepared to break the news that no, the bar was not open for another eight hours.

"Can't a person get a drink around here?" someone called out. Mallory blinked in shock and gave a cry as Becka Landon walked in.

"Oh my God, what are you doing here?" she cried, hustling across the room to give Becka a hug.

"And it's good to see you, too," Becka said dryly. She wore shorts and a T-shirt, both damp.

"Is it raining out?" Mallory asked.

Becka shook her head. "I've been running."

"You didn't jog here from Massachusetts, did you? I knew you were freaky about working out, but that's over the top even for you. Have a seat," she said, waving Becka to a stool and walking behind the bar to fill a glass with water. "There you are. On the house."

"Oh, the generosity of friends," Becka sighed, and gulped down half of it.

"So it's great to see you, but I'm still a little flummoxed. Are you staying here? Is Mace along?"

"Oh, he's here." Becka gave her a bright-eyed look and then relented. "We sailed down from Boston. We're on our honeymoon."

"What?" Mallory goggled.

Becka gave a laugh. "Honeymoon. Mace and I eloped a couple of days ago and we're taking his sailboat down to Florida and the Bahamas for our honeymoon."

Mallory looked at her like she was out of her mind. "You are aware that it's hurricane season, right?"

"Oh, that," Becka said flapping a hand. "It's the tail end and there are lots of good ports between here and Florida. We figure we'll take our time and stay at Mace's place for as long as we need to be sure the danger's past."

Mallory shook her head, trying to take it all in. "So back up to the eloped part. You're married?"

A smile spread over Becka's face like a sunrise as she held out a hand with a plain gold band. "The deed is done, baby."

"Congratulations." Mallory hopped up on the bar and slid to the other side to give Becka a hug. "That's great." She studied her. "You look happy."

"I am happy," Becka grinned. "Who'd have guessed?"

"Well, some of us sort of thought that if you stopped and thought about it for a minute you might just decide he was the one."

"Yeah, yeah, yeah. You and Stan, the matchmakers."

"I'd say we did a pretty damned good job, judging by the way you look," Mallory decided with a nod. She propped an elbow on the bar. "So why did you guys skip the whole wedding thing? Not that I blame you, but you both have families.''

Becka sighed. ''My mother is the original control freak. I saw what she did with my sisters' weddings. She would have made our lives miserable. It just made more sense to do it this way. I told everyone we were taking a couple of months off. When we come back, we'll just break the news and have a party for everyone. Of course, I may be disowned at that point,'' she added reflectively, ''but I'm sure she'll get over it. Mace has a way of charming her.''

''Mace has a way of charming everyone,'' Mallory told her. ''So you sailed here? I didn't know you knew how.''

''I didn't,'' Becka grinned. ''Mace taught me. He had a crew bring his boat up last month and we're taking it back down.''

''Where is he now?''

''Back at the boat doing all the port stuff. I just had to get off and go for a run. There's not a lot of room to move on a boat and I could feel myself turning into a puddle of mush.''

''Oh, yeah, I can see that happening,'' Mallory said dryly, her gaze flicking over the solid muscle of Becka's arms. ''Face it, Landon, you're a workout freak.''

''Someone's got to be,'' Becka said with dignity.

Mallory snorted. ''Nothing's worth working that hard over. I figure I'll just let nature take its course.''

Becka looked suspiciously at Mallory's sleek body. ''I still think you exercise on the sly.''

''In all my infinite spare time.''

''Speaking of which, how's the business?'' Becka

asked, turning to look around the space. "Things going okay?"

"We're covering expenses and starting to pay back the start-up costs, so yeah, things are going okay."

Becka glanced at her sports watch. "So are you booked up here? Why don't we go grab lunch somewhere outside and you can tell me all about it." She cleared her throat.

Mallory narrowed her eyes. "This wouldn't just be a ploy to get a free meal, would it?"

14

A COOL BREEZE WHISKED PAST them as they walked down the cobblestone street. Becka shivered. "I don't remember it being this cold when I was running."

Mallory threw her a sidelong look. "That's because you were in that disturbed jock frame of mind where you ignored it."

"Who, me?" Becka grinned. "So what's going on?"

"Work, mostly. Getting the business off the ground has been keeping me busy."

"It's succeeding, though? You're getting enough people through the door?"

"Are you kidding? We've been packed," Mallory said in satisfaction. "Ever since we started the bartenders dancing, we've had great numbers."

"Bartenders dancing? Those wouldn't be female bartenders, by any chance, would they?"

"With their clothes on," Mallory told her.

"Ah. Are you a big fan of *Coyote Ugly*?" Becka gave her an amused look.

Mallory shook her head. "It sort of happened by accident," she said lightly.

"How are your neighbors taking it?" Becka asked with interest.

Mallory shrugged. "I'm not violating any laws, so who cares? It's not the neighbors I'm worried about."

"What are you worried about?"

"Me? Nothing," she said, but a second too late. "Everything's fine and dandy."

Becka studied her. "Oh, you look just dandy. So bright and shiny you look like a candied apple."

"Like a candied apple?"

"Yeah, like you'd crack if I tapped you wrong."

Mallory's smile slipped. "What's that supposed to mean?"

"You tell me. Something's going on with you."

"Things are fine," Mallory said shortly.

Becka's eyes narrowed. "I'm sure," she said, sounding completely unconvinced. They walked a few steps farther and then she stopped short. "You know, the whole time we were friends in Lowell, you kept asking me about what was going on with Mace and I'd tell you, and it helped." Becka continued, "It didn't feel like prying. It's what friends do, but it goes both ways."

"I talked to you," Mallory protested.

"Oh sure, about work, opening the bar, that kind of thing." Becka waved it off. "You never talked about you, though. You never dated, you never said anything about how you felt about anything. And it looks like you still won't," she said, frustration shading her voice. "Something's obviously bothering you but all you can say is everything's fine." She fixed an uncompromising gaze on Mallory. "You don't get a prize for toughing it out alone. What you get is unhappy."

"What, are you people in some kind of club?" Mallory burst out. "You, Dev, Shay, all anyone can do is talk about me opening up. 'Tell us how you feel,' 'Let me in,' 'Open up, you'll feel better.' What a crock.

You spill your guts, you don't feel better. I'll tell you how you feel, you feel embarrassed and naked and really, really sorry you ever did it.'' She began walking again.

"Maybe." Becka looked up at the gulls circling over the harbor. "So who's Shay?"

"LET ME GET THIS STRAIGHT," Becka said as they sat in a booth at the Red Parrot. "Your brother comes in as your silent partner, then he gets a friend who lives here to check out your bar on the quiet and report back, and then he sics the friend on you as his watchdog?"

Mallory blinked. "That's pretty much it." She hadn't ever really had a girlfriend before. It surprised her how good it felt having someone take up her side and offer unquestioning support.

Becka scowled. "That is beyond out of line. I'd be pitching a royal fit."

"I suppose from Dev's point of view it's reasonable," Mallory reflected, taking a drink of her iced tea. "I mean, he's sunk a chunk of change into the bar and now he gets word that I'm doing something risky."

"Isn't he supposed to trust you?" Becka demanded.

Mallory traced patterns on the varnished wood of the tabletop. "It's complicated. I owe Dev so much. He's always been there for me. I couldn't have opened the bar without his backing, and he had every reason not to invest—he's got a business of his own."

"But he did," Becka pointed out. "He made a deal with you."

"Yeah," she sighed, "he did."

"So?"

"So sometimes I play things a little loose."

"If he didn't trust you, he shouldn't have gone into business with you," Becka countered.

A corner of Mallory's mouth tugged up. "You only have sisters, right?"

"Yeah. So?"

"Trust me, it's different. Dev's my big brother and he's always going to be looking out for me, and meddling a little, because that's what big brothers do."

"Then you're okay with this?"

"Resigned is more like it. I don't think he means any harm."

Becka digested that for a moment. "As long as you're okay with it," she said finally. "And your bartenders are dancing you into the black."

"That's one way of putting it."

"You know, I'd give my right arm to see you up there playing go-go girl," Becka said meditatively.

Mallory couldn't repress a smile. "I don't do it very often."

"Oh, yeah, but I bet when you do, you have 'em eating out of your hand."

The memory of dancing for Shay blinded Mallory for an instant. It flooded through her, the feel of moving for his pleasure, watching his eyes darken, watching his arousal build.

"Hello," Becka waved a hand in front of her. "Anybody in there?"

Just then, the waitress stopped at their table and Mallory breathed a silent thanks. "Let's see, I think I've got some lunch, here." With swift efficiency, she set their plates down, checked on additional requests, and left.

Becka spread a napkin in her lap and watched Mallory tuck into a plate of loaded potato skins. She shook her head. "Your veins must be filled with cholesterol soup."

"And you're going to have bean sprouts growing out your ears if you don't watch out," Mallory countered, dipping a bacon and cheese laden skin into sour cream before sinking her teeth into it with a sigh of pure bliss.

"Okay, so you're not ticked off at Dev and you're not stressing over the business," Becka said, forking up a bite of her veggie stir-fry. "But something's still bugging you."

Mallory glowered at her. "You're going to give me heartburn if you don't stop."

"Don't mind me, eat up." Becka waved at her genially. "I'm just thinking out loud here. If you're upset and it's not Dev or the business, then it has to be this Shay guy who's making you crazy," she said, with the air of someone who's solved a difficult math problem.

"La la la la, I can't hear you," Mallory said, fingers in her ears.

"Oh, yeah, you can."

Mallory dropped her hands and studied Becka. "You really are not going to let this go, are you?"

Becka shook her head. "No, I'm not. You didn't let me duck out last summer and I'm not going to let you now," she said soberly. "And let's be honest. If you really didn't want to talk about it, you'd have left me standing on the sidewalk when this first came up."

Mallory sighed and pushed her plate away. "Okay fine, it's Shay. Are you happy?"

"No way. Give me the rundown so I know what's going on and we can go from there."

Mallory gave her a half smile. "Are you part pit bull?"

"One quarter. Start talking," Becka ordered.

The tale took more time than Mallory had expected. By the end, they had migrated out of the restaurant and were sitting on Mallory's favorite bench overlooking the bay.

"Hmm. I'm going to have to get Mace to buy a motorcycle," Becka said reflectively. "So what's bothering you about it all?"

Mallory sighed. "It's complicated."

"That, it almost never is. Guy stuff usually falls into pretty easy categories. Girl has unrequited thing for guy. We can rule that out immediately," Becka decided. "No guy in his right mind would leave you unrequited."

"Gee, thanks."

"Thank your genetic donors," Becka advised. "Next, guy has unrequited or stalker thing for girl. Is Shay getting in your way?"

"No," Mallory sighed. "Shay's great, he just pushes for too much."

"Lifetime commitment?"

"Worse. He wants to get into my head. Like you," she said, with a stab at humor.

"And what do you want?"

"I don't know. We talked last night, late. I got upset." She squirmed at the memory. Even talking about it embarrassed her.

"How did Shay react? Some guys get weirded out when women get emotional."

Mallory shook her head. "It didn't bother him a bit. He was great."

"Well, that's good, then."

"No, that's just the problem. I wound up telling him things I never would have otherwise. Things I've never told anyone. He made it so easy it just seemed natural at the time, but when I woke up this morning I just wanted to crawl into a hole. And to make it worse, I realized that I—"

Becka's eyes softened. "That you what?"

"That I..." The words were too hard to say, too terrifying. "I care for him."

"Ah." Her tone said she understood all that Mallory couldn't say. "Now it all makes sense."

Mallory rubbed her temples. "I don't know how to handle this, Becka, I really don't. I don't know what I'm supposed to do. I don't know how to be someone's girlfriend. I don't know if I want to be."

"Darlin', it's kind of sounding like part of you has already made the decision. You don't have much of a choice."

"Sure I do." Her eyes glinted. "I just walk away and put it out of my mind."

Becka shook her head and gave a pitying smile. "Do you really think you can do that? Do you really think he'll let you?"

"It's not up to him!" she flared.

"And it's not just up to you, either," Becka reminded her. "There are two of you involved in this."

Mallory swallowed. "I'm really afraid, Becka. I feel like he's got all the power now and I've got none. I've given it to him with the things I've told him, with the things I feel. I just want to run."

"Where's this coming from? Listen to yourself. Relationships are about caring, not power."

"Of course they are," Mallory said impatiently. "You look at any relationship and there's one person who always cares more, and one person who controls. I see it with Dev and his fiancée, I saw it with my parents. And the person who loves more always surrenders ultimate control to the other person.''

"No." Absolute certainty filled Becka's voice. "Not always. Sometimes both people love enough that it isn't a question of degrees and power but just of making one another happy.''

"Says the new bride," Mallory said sardonically.

"I'm not embarrassed to believe in love," Becka returned. "The only thing that would shame me would be squandering it, having that ultimate gift and turning away. How do you feel about Shay? Cut the b.s. for a second, stop being scared, and just let yourself feel. What is the answer?''

A pelican soared in to land on a white-topped piling. Mallory watched as it clapped its beak a few times and settled in to get comfortable. She dropped her head into her hands. "God help me, Becka, I think I'm in love with him," she whispered. "What am I going to do?''

Becka reached out to squeeze her shoulder. "When I first realized I was in love with Mace it scared the hell out of me. It probably scares the hell out of everybody, don't you think?''

Mallory raised her head. "I don't like to think of myself as everybody.''

"Sorry, girlfriend. In this case, you're dumped in the stew with the rest of us." Humor danced in her eyes. "The thing is, once you find out that the guy feels the same way, it's okay. Then you're in it together.''

"Easy for you to say. You knew from the beginning

that Mace was stuck on you. How do I know what Shay feels?"

"Do you think it was easy for him to tell you he wanted more the other night? You don't think he was taking a chance laying himself out there?"

"I guess so," Mallory said.

"I'd say it's a pretty good guess he cares for you," Becka said thoughtfully. "That's you, by the way, not some image of you he has in his head. Otherwise, the less he knew about what you thought, the better. It sounds like he accepts you for who you are."

Mallory snorted. "Oh, yeah, right. He completely disapproves of the dancing. He's Mr. Conservative—"

"Who had sex with you on a motorcycle in a road-house parking lot," Becka put in.

"Yeah, but he's still got his Yankee values thing going. He thinks I'm being way too out there with the bar. It's like every other guy I've been with, they say they adore me and then they tell me I have to change."

"Has Shay ever actually told you to stop the dancing?" Becka asked curiously.

"Well, not in so many words. I know he disapproves. I know he'd like it if I stopped."

Becka shook her head. "That's not what I asked. He disapproves, Dev disapproves, but have either of them told you to stop what you're doing? Has Shay ever demanded that you change?"

"No," Mallory admitted reluctantly.

"And meanwhile he took you to meet his family, didn't he? That should tell you something right there. Trust me, just because you're in love with each other doesn't mean you always agree on everything. How boring would that be? Complete agreement is nothing, ultimately. But complete acceptance? That's everything.''

"So how do I know if that's what I've got?"

Becka shrugged. "Take a chance. Take it for a test drive and see how it feels. Only time will tell.''

BOATS BOBBED AT DOCKSIDE as they walked into the marina. Becka led the way toward the slip where *Squeeze Play* was docked. It was a sleek thirty-five-foot sloop with smooth lines and polished mahogany on the top. "Becka, it's gorgeous," Mallory breathed, staring at the sleek white boat.

Mace Duvall looked up from where he was polishing brightwork and waved. His sun-streaked hair was disheveled and hung over his eyes, which were an unusual warm brown the shade of aged whiskey.

"So's he," Becka replied with a little jitter to her voice. "My God, how did I ever get so lucky?"

"Afternoon, ladies," Mace drawled as they neared. "Don't just stand there, come on aboard."

Becka stepped from the dock to the boat and Mace immediately swung her into his arms, kissing her noisily.

"Stop it," she said, pushing at him halfheartedly. "We've got company."

"She understands," Mace said, glancing over at a grinning Mallory. "New husband prerogative."

Mallory stepped carefully onto the softly swaying boat and walked over to give Mace a hug. "Congratulations, Mr. Landon," she said, bussing him on the cheek. "You've got great taste in women."

"You've got it half right," Becka said, linking her fingers with Mace's. "I'm still Ms. Landon, he's still Mr. Duvall. It just seemed too weird to change my name at this point. I mean, I've had the name for almost thirty years.''

''You get no arguments from me,'' Mallory said.

''Saves getting a new driver's license and passport,'' Mace observed.

Becka grinned. ''I'm all for efficiency.''

''So give me the tour.''

It took longer than she expected to clamber over the boat. Mace had obviously gone first class when he'd bought it and kept it up—the mahogany deck and panels gleamed with soft luster, the sails were pristine white, the brightwork glittered. The belowdecks area was surprisingly roomy and cleverly designed to pack the most stuff into the least space.

''She's wonderful,'' Mallory said reverently.

''Sails like a dream, too,'' Mace said. ''We should get you out on the water while we're here.''

''Absolutely,'' Becka chimed in. ''What are you doing tomorrow? Better yet, what are you and Shay doing tomorrow?''

''Shay?'' Mace asked with interest.

''Mallory's new fellow.''

''Ah. Do I get to inspect him like an honorary big brother?''

''He's my big brother's friend, so he's already passed. Anyway, he's not my fellow,'' Mallory said quickly.

Becka rolled her eyes. ''You want me to say 'new friend' like my mother does?''

''Whoever he is, Mallory, invite him along,'' Mace said, fighting a grin. ''We can go out through the harbor and up the coast a bit.''

''I'll take care of lunch,'' Becka offered.

Mallory wrinkled her nose. "You're not going to feed us tofu burgers or anything like that, are you?"

"Not if she expects me to eat it, we won't," Mace said.

"I'm only trying to look out for your health," Becka said with dignity.

"I'd rather worry about my taste buds, thanks," Mallory returned. "Listen, thanks for the invite. Definitely count me in. I'll see if Shay can get loose and join us." She paused and gave Becka a suspicious look. "As long as you promise not to grill him."

"Who, us?" they said in concert, then grinned at each other.

Mallory rolled her eyes. "Oh God, you're already starting this married telepathy thing. What's next, baby and the baby carriage?"

Mace swept an arm around Becka and scooped her toward him. "Maybe," he said, grinning down at her. "Maybe."

SHAY SAT AT HIS DESK, trying without much success to concentrate on filling out orders for the following week. Normally he had them faxed in days ahead of deadline. This time around, he was just going to get in under the wire.

Assuming he got it done at all.

He blew out a breath of frustration. Ordering mixers and olives was about the last thing he cared about doing. What he wanted more than anything was to talk with Mallory, to find out just what the hell was going through her head.

When he'd awoken that morning, he'd reached for her and found only cool sheets. He'd looked for her and found only a note. It was one of the times he cursed his sense of responsibility. He'd wanted to scour the town until he found her; instead he'd found himself at O'Connor's doing prep and supervising.

Jumping to conclusions was a dangerous business, he reminded himself, but he couldn't shake the feeling that something was off. The night before, she'd opened up to him like never before, and she'd broken down. The disappearing act was no accident, he was certain. The question was how to keep her from bolting.

His first impulse was to find her and hold on to her, but it was no more appropriate than giving ultimatums. Now was the time he had to work hardest not to hold on but to leave it up to her. Besides, he couldn't do anything until he finished his overdue paperwork. He stifled his impatience and punched numbers into his calculator.

There was a knock on the door.

"Come in," he said brusquely.

The door swung open and Mallory walked in. Her loose, dark hair was beaded with mist, as was the raincoat she wore. She pushed the door closed behind her and looked at him. "Feel like taking a break?"

"Have a seat. There's a coatrack in the corner."

"I'll keep it on for now, thanks." Mallory dropped into the visitor's chair.

Shay looked at her steadily, drinking in the image. How was it that he hadn't even known she'd existed a month ago, and now so much of his world was centered on her? "I missed you this morning," he said softly.

Her eyes flickered to one side. "I figured I'd catch up with you later."

"And now here you are."

"Here I am," she agreed. A tension vibrated in her voice. It was subtle, but it put him on edge.

Mallory moistened her lips. "Look, I'm sorry I unloaded all that stuff on you last night. You were really wonderful about it."

Something tightened like a fist in his gut. "It wasn't a hardship. That's what you do when you care for someone."

"It's not something I'm in the habit of doing. You made it easy."

How could he tell her how much it meant that she'd trusted him enough to talk about it? Listening to her had torn at him, holding her while she'd wept had broken his heart. When they'd drifted off together, it had felt as though they'd fused together in some indefinable way. Waking alone had filled him with loss.

Mallory drew in a breath with the air of a soldier about to dive into the breach. "When I woke up this morning, I didn't know how to feel about it. I didn't know what to say to you. So I left."

He looked at her steadily. "I know."

She flushed. "This isn't easy for me, Shay. I did it wrong this morning, and I'll probably do it again. But I do care about you," she said desperately, staring into his eyes. "And I want this to keep going." There, she'd done it, she thought, her heart pounding as though she'd run a quarter mile.

Shay rose to circle around the desk to crouch in front of her. "You mean the world to me," he said simply, capturing her hands and bringing them to his lips. "I have no intention of doing without you."

"And what do you have the intention to do with me?" she asked, with a gleam in her eye, leaning in to press her mouth against his.

15

Advertising was a wonder, Mallory thought as she looked out over the people filling Bad Reputation. She'd been a little uneasy about losing money on the live music initially before it began paying for itself in cover charges or increased drinks sales. Now it looked like she'd worried for naught. She crossed over to check with Benny at the door.

"How we doing, Benny?"

"You should be a happy woman." he smiled. "We're at about three quarters capacity and climbing."

"Whatever you do, don't go over our max rating. If the fire marshal's going to stop by any night, it'll be tonight. We can't afford to get a violation."

"Don't worry, I'm keeping an eye on the numbers," he said with a wink, holding up his chrome hand counter. "Leave it to me, boss lady."

Before she could turn away, she heard her name called from the street and Fiona came walking up. Mallory whistled. Either Fiona had gone shopping or she had one hell of a secret life. The red mini she wore looked painted on, the skimpy camisole above it was patterned with silver shooting stars. Her red hair, always pulled back decorously now curled wildly down to the middle of her back. Silver stilettos gleamed on her feet, matching the long silver drops that twisted at her ears.

"Well, if you aren't a sight to behold," Mallory said.

"Is this sexy enough?" Fiona asked anxiously. "I wasn't sure what to wear."

"I don't know, Benny, is it sexy enough?" Mallory asked. "Benny?" Catching the poleaxed look on her doorman's face, she patted Fiona on the shoulder. "I think it'll work. Come on, I'll show you around."

Benny wasn't the only one who noticed the new and improved Fiona. The trip from the door to the bar took twice as long as normal, as half a dozen would-be swains tossed out lines. "Laugh and ignore it," Mallory instructed. "Remember the rules—no dating customers, no matter what. Flirt all you like, but it ends there."

"Got it," Fiona nodded, teetering on her heels. Finally they reached the walkthrough and ducked behind the bar.

"That's Belinda, Kayla, and Liane," Mallory said, pointing to the bartenders in succession. "We have two taps for each kind of beer, and the mixers are in the cabinets below the liquor. We keep the kegs in a cold room in the cellar. If you've got a tap that's running out, flag Randy, the guy in the Red Sox hat. He's our bar back, he'll take care of things."

Fiona smoothed down her skirt. "Well, time to start serving, then?"

Her words were drowned out by the whoops from the crowd as Kayla and Liane stepped up onto the bar to dance to Bonnie Raitt's "Let's Give 'Em Something to Talk About." Swinging their hips to the music, they prowled around one another, then strutted out to the far ends of the bar, playing the crowd, keeping time with their snapping fingers.

Fiona swallowed. "I don't have to do that, do I?"

Mallory laughed. "Hardly. Liane and Kayla are in a class of their own. You get up there and do whatever you like."

"So, is there, um, a schedule for dancing?" Fiona asked faintly.

Mallory shook her head. "No, just whenever the mood takes you. The steps to get up are over by the brass pole." She pointed, then took another look at Fiona's face. "Fee, there's nothing that says you have to do this. You've got a perfectly good job. You can even serve drinks here without dancing. The other three are hams enough they won't mind."

"No, really, I'm looking forward to it," Fiona said uneasily, eyes fixed on the dancing women and the crowd of men watching avidly from below. "Maybe I'll just watch a bit, first, though. I—" She did a double take and her smile slipped. "The band is playing tonight?" she asked hotly.

"Yes. Is that going to be a problem?"

Fiona stared at the bandstand. "No. I just thought it was next week is all. It'll be fine." She raised her chin. "Do I just go up on the bar?"

"Only if you're sure you want to. This isn't a test, you know."

"Oh, I want to," Fiona assured her, eyes suddenly bright as she turned to the stairs.

Mallory turned back to serving, fighting the sudden urge to plug her ears against the inevitable explosion.

COLIN UNROLLED THE EXTENSION cord to the wall and plugged it in. That was pretty much it, he figured, surveying the stage with his hands on his hips. Luckily they'd thought to set up the sound board earlier in the evening. With all the noise, there was no way they'd have been able to do a sound check.

A whoop from the bar area had him craning his neck around to see the source of the excitement. One of the perks of playing at a place like Bad Reputation was being able to watch gorgeous women dance all night, he thought. A guy could do worse than get paid for it.

He watched a mouthwatering redhead slide up and down the brass pole, teasing the crowd with her willowy body and her smile of promise. That one there, he thought. A man could get ridiculous over a face like that. He could find himself coming back night after night for the chance to imagine stripping the clothes off of her, of seeing her naked in bed wearing just that provocative smile.

A smile that looked familiar, now that he thought about it. A smile that held a hint of devilry, the same way as Fiona's did.

Fiona?

His eyes widened in shock.

SHE'D EXPECTED TO BE MORE nervous, with a roomful of people looking at her, but with the beat of the music drumming through her veins, she only felt sexy and confident. Making eye contact with one rapt face after another, she moved down the bar, now teasing, now tempting, now spinning away. As the music reached toward its climax, she shimmied her hips and lifted her hair up onto the crown of her head, eyes half closed in enjoyment.

"What in the hell do you think you're doing?" a voice roared at her.

Fiona's eyes snapped open. Red-faced and furious, Colin stood directly below her, staring up in outrage. She released her hair and spun then ran a hand over her hip, giving him a defiant look. As the song ended, she moved down the bar, leaving him behind even as the applause began.

"Good job, kid," Belinda called as she walked down the steps.

On the ground, Fiona began filling drink orders, her hands a blur of motion.

"I'm in love with you. Will you marry me?" asked a tall, lanky guy with an eyebrow ring.

"Oh, 'tis a fine offer but I'm sure I'm promised already," she said.

"And she's got an accent to boot. That shattering sound you just heard was my heart breaking," he said mournfully.

"How about a drink to numb the pain?" she said, with a wink.

"A shot of Glen Fidditch, then, in honor of your home."

"Well I'm Irish, not Scottish, but I'll take it as it's meant," she tossed back, setting a shot glass on the bar.

And then Colin was in front of her. "I want to talk to you," he snapped.

"That's funny," she said coolly, reaching for the bottle of Scotch. "I have absolutely no desire to talk with you."

"Hey pal, get in line, here," said her admirer.

Swiftly Colin moved behind the bar and tugged

Fiona's wrist to pull her into the back room. Her yelp of surprise was drowned out by the slamming of the door.

MALLORY STARED AT Fiona as she burst out of the back room. Twin spots of color burned in the girl's otherwise pale face.

"Are you okay?"

"Oh, it's splendid, I am," she snapped, stabbing viciously at the ice in the ice bin. "Why shouldn't I be, just because I've been humiliated by an idjit who doesn't want me but doesn't want anyone else to, either."

Her voice shook, with anger or anguish, Mallory couldn't tell. Sometimes one was practically the same thing as the other, she thought. Out of the corner of her eye, Mallory noticed Colin leave the back room and head toward the dance floor.

"Listen," she said, laying a sympathetic hand on Fiona's trembling shoulder. "We need some more popcorn for the snack bowl. You want to go in the back and make some?"

Fiona gave her a look filled with relief. "Thanks," she said gratefully.

A fine mess, Mallory thought, watching her go through the door to the back bar. Reminding herself that it was between Fiona and Colin didn't help. She'd known better than to hire Fiona, but then she'd found herself caught up in sympathy for the girl, who was every bit as trapped by stereotypes as she herself had been.

Mallory sighed. It was anyone's guess what Shay would think when he walked in later. For all that any reasonable bar owner knew that staff constantly hopped from establishment to establishment, she had a funny feeling that he would take Fiona's defection a little more personally. Granted, Fiona was still giving him full notice by working at O'Connor's while moonlighting for Mallory, but she was willing to bet that it still wouldn't set well. And she had a really funny feeling that he wouldn't take the sight of Fiona dancing any better than Colin had.

It was Fiona's decision, not theirs, she reminded herself. They'd get over it. It wasn't fair to Fiona to let their opinions and preferences control what happened to her. They could just learn to deal with it, she told herself firmly. Or maybe she could have a few words with Colin to calm him down, she thought.

Mallory ducked back out into the chaos. She tried to work her way over to the stage area, fighting through the press of bodies. Once she had a couple of minutes to calm Colin down, she was sure he'd see reason.

Before she could reach him, though, a few thumps from the bass drum had everyone looking up as the band launched into its opening number. The tune was catchy blues rock with an irresistible beat. Soon, bodies were crowded on the dance floor.

Mallory turned to head back to the bar, working her way between people and watching the band as she walked. They were really quite good, she thought as they wound up their first number and launched into something hooky but unfamiliar. An original? she wondered.

"Watch where you're going, idiot. You just spilled my beer!" Over near the bar, a group of rowdy frat boys had stumbled into a blue collar type, who'd been raptly watching Belinda dance. He was now glaring at the frat boys, and looked both older and brawnier than they did. That didn't stop the smallest of them, a scrappy, pugnacious redhead, from getting in his face.

Instantly Mallory stepped in.

"Hey, guys, hold it down, okay? I don't want to have to show you the street, so let's just relax and watch the band." Hoping her veiled threat sank home, she turned to the brawny guy. "If he spilled your beer, come on up to the bar and I'll get you a replacement."

The problem defused temporarily, Mallory craned her neck to find the bouncer and alert him to watch the group. The whole room was bobbing to the music now, a solid wall of people. She breathed a sigh of relief as she reached the walkthrough.

"Mallory," Belinda tapped her shoulder. "There's a leak in one of the keg lines. Randy's down in the basement looking at it."

"Damned rats," Mallory muttered as she hustled down to the cellar, all thoughts of finding the bouncer completely out of her head. She'd set out every kind of trap known to man, but they still came back, lured by the barley and malt scent of beer. Now, she and Randy would have to shut down the line, find the leak, and repair it before they'd be back in business. On a Saturday night, she wasn't taking chances.

Reaching and patching the leak in the line took Mallory's small hands, and far more time than necessary. Finally, sighing, she headed back upstairs to hear the lead singer's voice over the sound system. "This is the last song in our set. It's a special one, dedicated to the owner for giving us our first gig." The drummer clicked his sticks a couple of times and they launched into a blues rock version of Joan Jett's "Bad Reputation."

"I don't give a damn 'bout my reputation," the

singer growled, the rhythm section setting up an irresistible beat. "You're living in the past, it's a new generation."

"Come on," Fiona shouted in her ear. "This is for you, you have to dance to it." She dragged Mallory to the steps and pulled her up onto the bar.

The beat was sexy, relentless, and Mallory abandoned herself to it. The music flowed through her body and had her swinging her hips, bobbing her shoulders. Fiona danced and watched Colin. Grim-faced and driven, he played his guitar with a fury, pounding it until he snapped a string.

"You okay?" Mallory mouthed to Fiona, who gave a defiant nod, lifting her hair up and bumping to the thump of the bass.

"And I don't give a damn 'bout my bad reputation," Kayla, Mallory, and Fiona joined him in the chorus, to the cheers of the crowd. "Not me," they yelled, arms across one another's shoulders. "Not me." The last chord jangled just as the drums and bass cut.

Just as Shay walked in.

Mallory saw his eyes fasten on her, then on Fiona. He stopped in place, surprise flickering over his face. Frowning, he stepped back to lean against the wall ledge.

Her stomach muscles knotted up as she hurried down off the bar. Ducking through the walkthrough, she pushed her way across the room to Shay.

"Well isn't this a surprise," he said, looking over her shoulder at Fiona, who was dancing to the band's encore number. "Here I was guessing she'd wound up working for one of the other taverns."

"I planned to tell you," Mallory said quickly.

"And which of the five days we've seen each other since she gave notice were you planning to do that?" His gaze was flat, shutting her out.

Mallory pushed down the guilt that swamped her. "Come on, Shay," she said reasonably, "you've run a bar for fifteen years. You know staff comes and goes."

"Yes, indeed. They don't usually go to my lover's bar without anyone telling me, though," he said flatly.

"I didn't know if she wanted people to know. Things are delicate with Colin in the picture."

"Yeah?" An edge entered his voice. "Well, I'd say things are pretty damned delicate between you and me right now."

"Why, because you lost one of your people to me?" she flared.

"Because you didn't trust me enough to tell me what was going on. It's an important little word, trust." He gave her a hard look. "Without it, you don't have a hell of a lot of anything."

"Fiona was trusting me to keep confidence," she floundered.

"I guess you've got your priorities, then, don't you?" He scanned the room. "Look, we can talk about this later. Tell Col I'm sorry I missed the show. I have to get back to O'Connor's."

"Don't go away angry, Shay," she said, despising herself for pleading. This was what love did to you, she thought, reducing you to begging the one who was walking out the door.

"I'm not angry," he said shortly. "I'm disappointed. I'll get over it. Good night, Mallory."

She wouldn't feel guilty over it, Mallory told herself

as she watched him walk out the door. She turned to go back to the bar and suddenly uproar broke out.

''Don' tell me I can't get a fuckin' drink, bitch,'' a beefy blonde at the bar bellowed. He made a move to whirl around and she caught a glimpse of a knotted forehead and a nose that had been rearranged sometime in the past, before he stumbled into a group of young men.

''Watch where you're going, asshole!'' the scrappy redhead yelled. It was the frat boys again, she realized, kicking herself for getting distracted from calling in the bouncer earlier. Too much partying and weight-lifting had made the frat boys foolishly cocky, she realized as she muscled her way toward them. They were burly, but the drunk outweighed the redhead by an easy forty or fifty pounds.

''Stop it,'' Mallory shouted as they pushed and shoved. Just as she neared them, she saw a fist float through the air toward the drunk. Drunk he might have been, but he obviously knew how to fight, his battered features notwithstanding. He ducked the fist and responded with a punch that split the kid's eye open. Something warm and wet splattered over Mallory's face. She didn't want to think too much about what it might be.

What she wanted was to stop the fight in its tracks. Where were her damned bouncers? She looked wildly around to see Benny and Randy trying to reach her but blocked by the eager surge of the crowd, avidly watching the fight crash toward the bar. It was just a matter of time before someone really got hurt.

''Stop it,'' Mallory shouted, her words swallowed up in the roars and curses. ''We've called the cops.'' She launched herself at the drunk, trying to get to the pressure point in his neck before he could do any more damage. Instead, the spilled beer on the floor sent her slipping and falling against him. Someone screamed out her name.

"You trying to hit me?" the drunk snarled, grabbing her by the hair. He dragged her around in front of him and clamped a hand around her neck. Mallory fought, clawing at him, but her vision began to fog. When she saw him draw an arm back, she kicked at him, struggling to get loose.

Then he spun abruptly away and his face exploded into a fountain of blood as Shay rammed a fist into his face. Spots splattered onto Mallory as the drunk shook his head blindly and staggered.

"Goddammit, what are you doing in the middle of this?" Shay shouted and shoved her toward the bar. "Go." When he turned back, the drunk was waiting for him with a looping roundhouse punch. Shay managed to duck most of it, but even the partial contact made him see stars. Get back and below the punch, he thought, and danced around his opponent, who punched at thin air, looking increasingly befuddled. When the drunk dropped his guard just a little, Shay saw his moment and stepped in with a sharp uppercut.

The man's head snapped back and his teeth clacked sharply together. Then, with a surprisingly graceful turn, he dropped to the floor and began snoring.

16

"ARE YOU ALL RIGHT?" Mallory stood in front of Shay, blood splattered over her face and soaking into the white of her shirt.

"Jesus, where are you hurt?" he demanded, afraid to touch her. "What did he do to you?" And why had he stood by all these days while she continued to tempt fate, teasing and goading the roomful of men until one of them decided not to take no for an answer?

"I'm all right, Shay." She put her hands on his shoulders. "It's not my blood," she repeated until he finally registered what the pattern of sounds meant.

It still ran through his head in an endless loop, the shouts that had brought him back to the bar, the sound of someone screaming Mallory's name, the sight of the enormous tank of a man aiming his fist at her face.

The adrenaline-charged panic of not knowing whether he could reach her in time.

The sick fear still rolled in Shay's gut. Just the glancing blow he'd taken from the man's fist was enough to have the entire side of his head throbbing. Who knew what a straight-on punch might have done to her?

"Come on, everybody, we're supposed to be having fun here," Belinda shouted into the thinned-out crowd. Someone turned the jukebox up and Shay stared around the bar in exasperation. Night after night, they pushed the wild party atmosphere. Was it any wonder it had finally gotten out of control? The only thing he was sure of was that it had to stop, now, before someone got seriously hurt. Before anything happened to Mallory.

And if it took him stepping in and playing the heavy to make it happen, that was just too bad.

"Your poor face," Mallory murmured, touching the already puffy cheekbone with her fingertips.

Shay moved his head away. "Leave it."

"And your hand, too." His breath hissed in when she lifted it to examine his split and bruised knuckles. "We should wash and bandage that," she said.

"Later," he said brusquely, trying to ignore the smear of blood on her cheekbone.

"It's got to be hurting," she protested.

"Forget it," he snapped. In actual fact, it was throbbing like a mother, but it was inconsequential. "We need to have a serious talk. Now."

She blinked, finally registering his irritation. "Fine," she said curtly, matching his tone. "Let's go in the back."

On her way through the bar, she filled a clean cloth with ice and slapped it into his good hand with unnecessary force. "Put it against your cheek."

He gave her a stormy look, but obeyed.

In the back bar, Mallory leaned against the counter by the door and crossed her arms. "You mind telling me what the problem is?"

"You really don't know?"

"Don't waste time getting cute, Shay," she said impatiently. "If you want an apology, fine. I'm sorry you got hurt, truly, and I'm grateful you got me out of a jam, but we have bouncers for that. I've got people I pay to get hurt. You didn't need to do it.''

The throbbing pain and residual fear catalyzed into fury. ''Goddammit, Mallory,'' he exploded, ''I don't care about getting hurt. I came back in here tonight and found you covered in blood and about a second away from getting your lights punched out by a six-foot-five gorilla.''

She stayed toe to toe with him. ''It wasn't my blood.''

''What does it matter? Are you just willfully not seeing this? If that guy had hit you, he could have fractured your jaw or your cheekbone, or worse. You're asking for it with the atmosphere and with the way you're running this bar. That guy was hammered and your bartenders had no business serving him, no business at all.''

''My bartenders know better than to serve drunks,'' she said hotly.

''Yeah, well maybe you were all too busy teasing the crowd to notice.''

''Teasing?'' she repeated slowly, something flickering in her eyes.

''What did he do, was he watching you? Did he try something, is that what got all of this started?''

''Watch it, Shay,'' she warned him. ''You don't know what you're talking about.''

He knew, all right. Hadn't he imagined it? Hadn't he seen her lying broken in the seconds it took him to trample over everyone in his way so he could get to her? ''I'm not the one who doesn't have sense enough to realize you don't tease idiots until they're fighting to get to you.''

Her voice was like ice, frigid and emotionless. "You've got it all wrong."

If ice ran through Mallory, fire ran through Shay. "No, you've got it all wrong," he said, raising his voice again. "When are you going to wake up and realize that every single night you're up there getting cute, you've got yourself a room full of TNT? Sooner or later someone's going to get stupid enough to come after you, like that idiot did tonight. Do you love it so much, being the bad girl, that you're willing to risk people's safety?"

"I'm not risking anyone," she protested.

"Yes, you are. It's my fault, too. Your brother sent me in here to look after you, and instead I've been standing around letting this go on."

Time stopped for an instant. "What did you say? Letting this go on? What, letting me run my business?"

"I meant—"

"I don't give a damn what you meant," she said furiously. "I run my business my way."

"Sure, and we all sit and watch you up there."

It was like a fist suddenly tightening around her chest, making it hard to breathe. "What, are you ashamed, Shay? I seem to remember you out there watching not so long ago, or were you just slumming it?" She tried to swallow the bitter taste at the back of her throat. It didn't matter what he said, she told herself fiercely.

"That was between you and I. This is between you and everyone." His eyes burned at her. "Wasn't tonight enough to make you realize you're not just risking yourself, you're risking other people? I should have put my foot down a long time ago."

"Like hell. You don't put your foot down here. This isn't O'Connor's. Bad Reputation is *mine*."

"Jesus, Mallory, clue in. I'm not talking about territory. I'm talking about taking care of the people who work here, which is what a responsible boss does." His words were scathing. "I thought that was important to you, but it apparently doesn't even register on your list of priorities."

"My priority is running a business."

"You're doing this to make a point, and maybe because you enjoy rubbing everyone's nose in it. Does it really mean that much to you to laugh at them all, to be Mallory the bad girl, who never bows to convention?"

Let me in, he'd said, and she had. And now she had nothing to protect her from the bolts he hurled. "I'm trying to take care of people, including Dev," she managed to say.

"Dev doesn't expect you to put yourself up there like a piece of meat to bring in customers. You're doing this for your own ego. Except that now you're risking yourself and everyone else to be able to say you've won."

"It's making the bar work," she said over the roaring in her ears.

"It's shortsighted and irresponsible. When you've got people working for you, you've got to think of them first and foremost. If you don't, then you're no good, not as a manager, anyway. You're just being selfish."

It was like being sliced with a razor sharp knife, so quickly that she didn't feel the pain, just looked down to find blood streaming from a fatal wound. *You're a selfish girl, just like your no-good mother,* she heard her aunt's voice. Shay's words shivered through her and anger condensed into a choking cloud of hurt.

How could she have been fool enough to think he'd accept her and care for her?

"It's got to end," Shay said. "Now."

She looked at him suddenly, her eyes blazing in a pale face. "I'll tell you what's ending," she flung at him. "You and me. Now get the hell out of my bar."

She whirled and slammed out of the back room, making Fiona jump where she was pouring drinks. "God, Mallory, you're white as a ghost. What's happened?"

Don't think about it, Mallory told herself, ignoring Fiona to duck under the walkthrough. She had to get out before Shay came after her. Before she broke down completely.

She stopped Belinda on her way back to the bar with a load of empty glasses. "Can you close up tonight? I have to leave."

"On a Saturday night?" Belinda's voice was rich with surprise. "You never leave on a Saturday night."

"Something's come up. Can you do it?"

"Yeah, sure." Belinda took a closer look at her. "Are you okay? That bruiser muscled you around some."

Not nearly as much as Shay just had. "I'm fine. Just take care of things." The less she said, the better.

"Okay. See you tomorrow."

Mallory didn't answer, just walked away. The thing to do was to concentrate. If she concentrated on getting up the stairs and into her apartment, she could keep it together. She wouldn't crumble until she was in her private space where no one could see her. A breath of cool air whisked through the front door and her grip on her control slipped a notch. She opened the door to her stairs and put her foot on the bottom tread.

"Mallory!" The voice came from behind her.

She turned to see Fiona.

"Are you okay? Where are you going?"

"I'm fine," Mallory said, looking beyond her to see Shay walking out of the back room. Her voice felt unsteady and she pitched it lower. "Belinda's going to handle closing up."

"What's wrong?" Fiona stepped closer.

"Nothing," she said, and to her horror her voice shook. She whirled and ran to the stairs that led to her apartment, leaving Fiona behind her.

Fiona stood for a moment in shock. It took more than the sight of blood to rattle a woman like Mallory, more than getting shoved around a little.

It took a man.

Fiona turned and saw Colin standing near the bar, holding on to Shay's arm to keep him from coming toward her. Toward Mallory.

Temper began to drum through her. She'd heard only snatches of their fight from the back room, but it didn't take much to put two and two together. She stalked toward them.

"Fee."

Colin started reaching out for her and she whirled on him furiously. "You keep your hands off me, Colin O'Connor. You've no right to me, none at all. And you, Shay," she said, glaring at him. "What did you say to Mallory to upset her?"

"That's between her and me."

"Well, you were yelling at her loud enough to include a few more of us. You pulled out all the stops, didn't you? What is it with you O'Connors?'' She stared from one to the other furiously. ''What, did you think that lummox was trying to hit Mallory because she wouldn't go along with him?''

The tightening of Shay's jaw told her she'd hit the mark. ''Bloody hell, both of you, you just decide who you want people to be without even taking a look. Did you ever ask Mallory what happened? Did you ever think to?''

''I already know—''

''You don't know anything,'' she said grimly. ''It might interest you to know that you're dead wrong. That big lug wasn't trying to paw her. You didn't barge in and save her virtue in spite of her reckless ways. It was a bar fight, plain and simple. It had nothing to do with Mallory.''

''He had his hands on her,'' Shay insisted stubbornly.

''Too right, he did. And in case you hadn't noticed when he collapsed on you, he's blind drunk. Blurs, that's all he's seeing.'' She threw Shay a furious look. ''I was up on the bar dancing, I saw the whole thing. The drunk jerk bumped into the college boys. They were in a mood and one of them took a swing.''

''Big mistake.'' Shay flexed his battered hand and winced. ''He knew how to fight, even as drunk as he was.''

''Mallory saw it, too. She tried to get him in a comealong but he was too tall for her and then he just had her.''

He shook his head, trying to ward off the image.

Fiona saw him and softened just a bit. ''It could have happened anywhere. Mallory was just trying to break it up. It didn't matter about the dancing. It'd be a miracle if he even realized she was a woman.''

All the fury bled out of him. He'd wanted it to be the dancing. He'd wanted a reason to end it, he thought, staring around the half-empty bar. He was afraid for her. It was the one thing he hadn't said, he realized, the most important thing of all. He hadn't told her that his heart had practically stopped during the fight. He hadn't said that she was all that mattered to him. He'd never told her he loved her.

"Where did she go?" he asked softly.

Fiona gave him a disdainful look. "Oh, now you're asking questions," she said, but she saw the lines of strain in his face and relented. "I think she went up to her apartment to change. She was headed toward her stairs, anyway, when I saw her last."

Shay turned and walked toward Mallory's stairs without a word.

"Remind me never to make you mad," Colin said as she started to pass him.

"What makes you think you haven't already," she said tartly, stopping to look at him.

"Me? What have I done?"

She stepped in front of him. "You're as big a fool as your brother, making your assumptions, sticking people into little boxes."

"Like who?"

"Like me," she retorted, then cut him off before he could say a word. "And if you value your family jewels, don't you dare tell me I'm like a sister to you," she said, her voice low and venomous.

He stared at her and then, to her infinite surprise, he began to chuckle. "No, Fee, after tonight I'm never going to think of you like a sister again."

"Don't laugh at me," she ordered him, but her mouth softened.

"Ah, Fee, I can understand why Shay flew off the handle tonight," he said soberly. "He was scared as hell, and I understand because I was too. When I saw that fight move toward the bar, I just knew that some idiot was going to knock you off in the middle of everything."

"I've enough sense to look out for myself," she returned.

He shook his head. "Doesn't matter. When someone you care about is at risk, you're always afraid of the worst." He reached out to curl his fingers around her upper arms. "I couldn't believe my eyes tonight when I saw you up there. Gorgeous, sexy enough to drive me nuts. I've never wanted anyone like that, never." His hands slid down her arms to hold her hands. "And then I realized that it was you, my buddy, and I didn't know how to make those two things mix." His hands tightened on hers.

"And what do you think now?" Her voice was soft and shook just a bit.

"I think if I can get the woman on the bar and my buddy all in the same package, I'd be one damned lucky guy. What do you think?"

She leaned in toward him and his arms slipped around her. "I think I might just be the lucky one." She pressed her mouth against his.

Quick footsteps hurried up to them and Shay stood there.

"She's gone."

17

A BODY IN MOTION STAYS in motion, so Newton said. She'd stepped gently up the stairs as though if she let her feet come down too hard she'd shatter the fragile bubble that protected her. Pausing in her apartment had seemed untenable; only moving kept the anguish circling around her at bay. Without even pausing for thought, she'd found herself purse in hand, walking down her back stairs and opening the door to her truck.

She'd been on the highway out of town before she'd realized it. If she concentrated on moving, she wouldn't have to remember the words Shay had flung at her, she wouldn't have to remember the way she had felt the moment she realized that it was over.

But where to go, that was the question. What was she going to do, show up on Dev's doorstep and explain the whole mess? Go back to her place, where the very walls would be echoing with her gullibility? Or just leave it all behind, find her way to another town?

The idea beckoned her. Escape, forget that she'd ever believed in Shay, that she ever dropped her defenses so that he could get inside and tear her to the ground. Forget that she'd forgotten all the lessons of her life and let herself love.

It was seductive, nearly irresistible. And, she realized with a rush of panic, nearly impossible. She was tied to a business now. She could throw away her own investment; she couldn't throw away Dev's. A greasy wave of desperation flowed through her. All she wanted to do was leave, and for the first time in her life she couldn't. Not without leaving ruin behind.

The highway stretched out in front of her headlights as she drove. She had to go back, she knew it. She had to turn around. Still, she was four hours along the New York State Thruway before she could make herself pull into a rest area.

The big, barnlike facility was still unlocked, though the inside lights were dim and the fast food joints shuttered. Her footsteps on the tile echoed as she crossed to the facilities. She stopped to wash her hands on the way out of the deserted rest room. Reaching for a paper towel from the dispenser under the mirror, she caught a glimpse of herself and froze in shock.

Under the pitiless glare of the fluorescent lights, her haunted eyes stared back at her from a face that was pale with exhaustion. Garish spots of blood spattered her white T-shirt; a smear of it ran along one cheekbone.

She wanted to shy away from the beaten-looking stranger in the mirror, she wanted to flee from anyone who knew her. More than anything, she wanted to stay moving and never go back. The thought of talking to Shay, even seeing him, made her stomach churn. She'd thought he'd cared for her, that he'd accepted her. How could she have been so wrong? And how could she now be trapped, unable to escape an untenable situation?

Mallory leaned her hands on the sink, the white porcelain cool and smooth against her fingers. Had her mother felt like this, filled with this desperate desire to escape? Maybe she hadn't planned to leave. Maybe the pressure, the fights had just mounted up until one day she'd started moving and had simply lacked the strength to make herself stop.

Returning to do what was necessary took courage. The suffocating weight of responsibility Mallory felt made her want to run all the more, even as she knew she couldn't. Had that been the way her mother had felt about their family? Were Mallory and Dev a crushing duty that she just couldn't tolerate any more? Was she so stifled that fleeing was preferable to staying, even though she'd had to know the damage she would leave in her wake? And what did that say about her, Mallory, that she found herself at the same juncture?

You're selfish. You're no good. You're just like your mother, the voice chanted in her head.

Her eyelids prickled. The image in front of her blurred, though she blinked to drive the tears away. For an instant, she saw her mother in the wavery, blurred face in the mirror. And for an instant Mallory understood the emotions and fears that had raged through the woman who had abandoned them. And now, on a rain-soaked turnpike three hundred miles from home, Mallory faced her mother's choice.

Slowly her knees folded and she sat on the mottled blue-green tile and wept.

WHERE WAS SHE? The question drummed through Shay's mind without respite. Her truck was gone. He'd found her doors unlocked and her cell phone on the counter; only her purse was missing. She'd told no one where she was headed.

He didn't find her out at the roadhouse, she wasn't

at O'Connor's, and she sure as hell wasn't in Bad Reputation. He fought the temptation to camp out at the base of her stairs. Dev's, he finally decided, she had to have gone to Dev's.

He checked his watch, knowing he was needed at O'Connor's. If she'd headed out immediately after their fight, she'd reach Dev's after one or two in the morning. There was no point in calling until morning.

So he told himself later at O'Connor's as he paced behind the bar and stared restlessly at the phone. If she'd been angry with him, he'd have been happy of the opportunity to let her cool down before they talked. Instead he remembered the dark, haunted look that flickered in her eyes before she walked out. Why had he talked about everything but what she meant to him? He poured drinks and tried not to stare at the clock as nine became eleven and eleven became midnight, and one day gave way to the next.

When the phone rang, he pounced on the receiver, hope sprinting through him. "Hello?" he asked, already thinking of what he would say to Mallory if it was her.

"Man, you blew it big time." Dev's voice blasted out of the phone. "What the hell were you thinking?"

Shay squeezed his eyes shut. He'd give Dev his pound of flesh later, but now he needed to talk to Mallory. "I don't really want to get into it right now, Dev."

"I bet you don't," Dev returned. "How you could miss the blues festival of the year because you had to work is beyond me. What kind of a music fan are you?"

Shay blinked at his reflection in the mirror behind the bar as Dev's string of good-natured insults slowly registered. The man should have been leaping down his throat over Mallory, not harassing him about a missed concert. Which meant that he didn't know. She would have been there by now, and Dev would have needed only a glance to know there was something wrong.

Mallory hadn't gone to him. She had to be back at her apartment.

Belatedly Shay tuned back into Dev's diatribe. "What are you doing calling so late?"

"We just got in. I wanted to rub your nose in it."

Shay stifled his impatience and tried to sound casual. The last thing he wanted was Dev figuring out something was wrong. "We'll settle up next time I see you. We're going to be closing soon, though. I've got to go. You can call and gloat tomorrow."

"You can bet I'll do that. Say hi to Mal for me."

If he only could, Shay thought.

THE CLATTER OF THE NEWSPAPER delivery truck woke Shay from the uneasy doze that had claimed him after he'd come home from O'Connor's. In just that instant, sleep was banished for good. Sighing, he rose and dressed. Maybe a walk would help wear away the tension that had him strung taut as a wire.

Outside, the streets were chill and dry, the sky flushed with the pink light of dawn. When his feet made the turn to Washington Square, he gave a wry smirk at himself. Like there was any doubt about where he was really going. He wasn't prepared to wait any more, even if it was early. She could sleep after he had said his piece. There were things she needed to know before any more time went by. They needed each other, he thought as he turned into the alley that ran behind her building.

He was four or five steps up the back stairs before he registered the fact that her truck was still missing from the parking bay. When he reached the top landing and peeked through the window into her kitchen, he saw a scene unchanged from the night before.

One by one, the hairs on the back of his neck prickled up. By the look of things she'd been gone all night. She wasn't at Dev's, Becka and Mace had long since sailed away. Where was she?

She probably just needed time, he told himself as he walked slowly down the stairs trying to quell his apprehension. Someone would have called Dev by now if she'd wound up in the hospital, and Dev would have called him.

It wasn't the first time she'd bolted on him. It was too soon to be concerned, definitely too soon to call out the dogs. Mallory would be back that afternoon for bar prep, he was sure of it.

But deep in his gut, an icy ball of anxiety began to form.

A CHILL DAWN BREEZE BLEW IN off the water as the rising sun lit the rocks below the Cliff Walk. Mallory shivered and pulled her coat more tightly around her. She'd found the thin jacket in the cab of her truck, along with a pair of tennis shoes to replace her stilettos. It wasn't ideal, but it was the best she had. She needed to be out and she needed to be moving.

The ebb and flow of the waves was hypnotic, rushing in and around the rocks, then flowing away. A piece of cork float, broken away from who knew where, bobbed on the surface. She watched as the waves caught it up and pounded it against the rocks. Then it disappeared beneath a boiling mass of whitewater. When the wave receded, the float bobbed back up and followed the sucking water, only to be pounded back into the rocks on the next surge.

She knew how it felt. Impossible to realize that just a day or two before, things had been right in her world. She'd been in love, bobbing on a wave of joy. Then, in a moment, all had turned. Like the cork getting pounded into the rocks, she'd been battered by Shay's condemnation, by the sudden realization that he didn't accept her, didn't care for her. Her love for him had left her with no defenses. She only felt battered, sucked under into a churning confusion of emotional whitewater in which she couldn't breathe or think.

Running hadn't helped. All across the miles of highway, it had traveled with her. Turning around had been the hardest thing she'd ever done, but ultimately, it had been her only real choice. The storm of weeping had left her drained but clear of purpose—her mother's path was not for her. She understood, now, in a way she never had. Forgiveness was too much to try for at present, but perhaps some day. For now, it was enough to have cast aside the grief she'd carried for so long.

Ultimately the water had drawn her, as it always had. Going back to her apartment was a bit more than she could face. Maybe the comforting rhythm of the waves would help her rebuild her defenses so that she could face Shay, if need be, without crumbling.

She rose and began walking, her feet scrunching on the dirt of the trail. How did you do it, she wondered, how did you forget and go on? In some small way she could understand her father drinking himself into oblivion all their lives. If she'd never known what it was like to love and be loved back, she'd never have missed it. False though the feeling might have been, it left a gaping hole behind.

Stooping, she seized a small rock lying at the side of the trail and threw it toward the water. Then she grabbed another, and another. Suddenly she was scrabbling for rocks and heaving them in a frenzy, the bursts of violence an outlet for the turmoil in her mind.

Breathing hard, she whirled around to find more rocks. Then she noticed the figure walking toward her. Recognition took only an instant.

Adrenaline spiked through her veins, and with it came a sudden strengthening of purpose. He wouldn't run roughshod over her as he had the night before, she resolved, squaring her shoulders, pushing the misery aside. She had more fortitude than either of her parents, and what had destroyed them would not take her down. What was necessary, she would do, she told herself. What she had to survive, she would survive. And after it was over, she would go on.

If she didn't splinter into a million pieces.

As Shay neared, she saw the light of resolve in his eyes. The golden morning light made him look very young.

He came to a stop in front of her, his breath coming out in white puffs of condensation. "I've been worried about you," he blurted, hands balled in his jacket pockets.

She congratulated herself on her dismissive shrug. "Forget it. It's over."

"I don't want to forget it."

Casual evaporated in an instant. "I don't think

that's up to you, Shay," she said curtly. "You had your chance to talk last night. That's all you get."

"No."

It welled up, then, the misery. "What, you want to yell some more? You want to tell me I don't know what I'm doing? That I'm selfish and irresponsible? You were the one who kept saying open up, let me in. Sorry, buddy, I'm not a fool." She turned and walked blindly away from him, down the trail.

He caught her in a few steps, touching her on the shoulder. "Turn around and look at me. Just give me a minute."

It was the note of pleading that did it. Pleading from a man unused to it. Unwillingly she turned to face him.

He swallowed. "When I came into the bar last night and saw that ox getting ready to punch you, it scared the hell out of me. All I could think is that he was going to hurt you, really hurt you, and I couldn't stop him."

"It wasn't your responsibility—" she began.

"Stop, okay? Just let me get through this." He raked his hair out of his eyes and drew a breath. "All I could think when I was fighting to get to you was that I had never really told you how I felt. I never told you that I'm in love with you."

She heard the rush of the waves, the cry of a shore bird. And over and over, his words shivered in her mind. In love with her? Shay? Her first reaction was elation, followed closely by doubt and fear. The night before was too fresh in her mind.

Shay shook his head, his face twisted in self-disgust. "I was so busy being afraid for you that even after everything was all right, I wasn't thinking clearly. I don't want you to do things that put you at risk because I don't ever want anything to happen to you. But I didn't cut through all the crap about the bar to make that clear to you. I was an idiot.'' He reached out and touched her cheek. ''Mallory, I love you so much. I was going crazy last night when I didn't know where you were. You mean everything to me.''

She could only look at him, caught in turmoil.

Shay stared at her. ''Look, you might not be ready to hear this right now. I probably didn't have the right to say those words to you, but I needed you to hear them. I don't know if you want me now or not, but I need you. Be with me, Mallory,'' he said softly.

''Shay, I…'' she faltered.

Determination lit his eyes. ''If you need time, you need it, but I warn you, I'm going to be very hard to get rid of. I'm going to convince you we're right for each other if it's the last thing I do.''

''You don't have to,'' she whispered, swallowing hard.

''What?'' He leaned in to hear her.

Her heart rabbited in her chest. Take the risk or shut it down? She could live like she had been for twenty-nine years. Or she could trust Shay and his parents, trust Becka, trust Dev that relationships could be more than the wasteland that had been branded in her consciousness as a child. ''You don't have to convince me,'' she said more loudly. ''I'm…'' She hesitated. ''I'm in love with you.''

Relief, wonder and joy chased across his features. Then he crushed his mouth on hers. ''Can you say that again, please?'' he asked, breaking away for a breathless moment. ''I didn't quite hear it.''

Mallory laughed, buoyed by a sudden lightness. ''I'm in love with you.'' It was easier the second time, she discovered. "I've known it since the morning we woke up together."

"The morning you bolted," he clarified.

She flushed. "It's not easy when you first realize it," she said.

He tightened his arms around her and brushed her lips with his. "I hear that. I had to get it knocked through my head by your brother."

She raised her eyebrows. "Dev knows?"

"Are you kidding? He was the one who told me what was going on."

She laughed, suddenly giddy, and leaned in for a long, lingering kiss. "I think we should go back to someplace with a bed and celebrate properly," she said.

"You'll get no arguments from me." He grinned. He released her and they began to walk back toward the nearest exit. The sun was fully up over the water now, brightening into day.

"Shay," Mallory said, tangling her fingers with his. "We need to talk about the dancing..."

"The dancing isn't an issue, okay? It's your bar and it's your choice. I'm always going to want to take care of you because that's who I am. But you've got to be who you are, too."

"When I was driving around last night, I thought a lot about the fight and about what you said. You're right, the dancing is getting to be too much. As of today, it's over."

"Are you sure?"

She nodded. "Yes, I'm sure." She sighed and stared at the trail ahead. "I just wish I knew how we'd guarantee a full house." Their feet crunched on the dead leaves that had blown onto the trail.

"You managed to pack in a pretty full house the other night, with the additional draw of Colin's band," Shay said thoughtfully.

"We got a great turnout, at least until the fight cleared things out."

He nodded. "I think I told you this town needs a good live-music club. Something more edgy than the folk we get in at O'Connor's and the jazz bars. Wouldn't Bad Reputation be the perfect spot for it?"

"Now there's an idea. I don't know anything about booking, though."

"I could act as your booking agent," he offered.

She tipped her head, considering. "Are you talking about a partnership?"

"Well, I don't know," he said, narrowing his eyes. "Partnerships can be challenging."

"Not if you have a legal agreement," she argued.

He thought about it. "Nah, I don't like it. Being in business with family is one thing. Being in business with a lover is a lot more chancy. I mean, what if we broke up, then we'd have to deal with untangling the business arrangement."

"I supposed it could be a problem," she said, a little flutter of nerves in her stomach. "Maybe we should just forget about it." Maybe he wasn't so sure about her after all, she thought with a twist of anxiety.

"Wait a minute." Shay stopped and pulled her around to face him, his hands on her hips. "Don't get me wrong, as far as I'm concerned, I'm crazy in love with you and always will be. I'm just saying that I'm not used to working outside of the family."

"Like I said, let's just keep business and pleasure separate." Her voice tightened.

"I suppose we could." He mulled it over. "But then maybe there's another solution."

"What's that?"

Humor slipped into his eyes. "I could just make you into family."

"Me? In the O'Connor clan?" She fought a smile.

"Purely for business reasons, of course," he hastened to add.

"Of course," she agreed.

"The fact that we'd get to have wild sex on demand would merely be an added benefit."

"Sure."

"And the fact that I adore you unreasonably would just simplify the arrangement."

"Naturally."

"So will you marry me?"

She eyed him. "Wild sex on demand?"

"Guaranteed."

She leaned in so that her mouth hovered a fraction of an inch above his. "It's a deal, partner. I think the O'Connor clan could use another go-go dancer."

"What do you mean?" he asked, startled.

Her laugh was rich and light. "I'll tell you in bed."

* * * * *

Let the luck continue...
Author Kristin Hardy's miniseries
UNDER THE COVERS
concludes in July 2003
with
SLIPPERY WHEN WET
Turn to the next page for an excerpt.
Don't miss it!

1

EXOTIC BIRDS HOOTED as Taylor walked along the flagstone path that wove through the lush jungle of the Iberonova resort. On either side of the jungle lay the brightly colored stucco huts that housed the hundreds of guests, but you'd never know it. From the winding path that led through the center of the resort to the beach, she could see only vines, trees bearded with Spanish moss, monkeys, and the occasional bird.

She emerged at the edge of the enormous, curving free-form pool with its central stone fountain spraying droplets of water that glittered in the sun. Around the edge, guests sprawled on lounges under umbrellas, dozing or reading or sipping exotic drinks. Funny how some people would come so far only to lie around a pool, as they probably could at home. What Taylor wanted was the beach.

Ahead, a pair of parallel walls of warm golden stone rose higher than a man's head. On their inner surfaces, a series of carved stone faces with Mayan features stared impassively at one another. Water gushed out of their full lips at the turn of a tap, and out of the fluted funnels below them. The guest showers, she realized, watching a young girl wash off her feet.

Ahead of her, curving palm trees framed the view of an ocean that stretched out an impossible shade of aqua, darkening to indigo on the horizon. A white catamaran with a sail banded in turquoise, blue green, and hot pink glided over the waves.

A smile spread across Taylor's face.

For two weeks, she'd been hopping from island to island, resort to resort, sometimes touring three or four properties in a day. Every night, she was somewhere different, never anywhere long enough to relax. It wasn't about relaxing, though. It was for her travel agency. Admittedly, it was work that she enjoyed, but work nevertheless.

This week, though, this was her time. Seven precious days to herself, to sleep, read, lie on the beach and do absolutely nothing that she didn't want to do. She picked up her straw bag and started down the broad beach.

As she walked past the sun worshippers, she relaxed to hear the mix of languages. No Texas twangs or nasal Yankee accents talking about PTA meetings and sports here. The mix of French, Italian, German and Spanish danced in her ears. Perhaps they were talking about the banal, but with the musical flow of syllables, it hardly mattered. Americans were outside the norm, here.

In fact, most of the European and South American women here had matter-of-factly dropped top when they hit the beach. Taylor set her straw bag in the shade of a palapa, pulling over a sun couch. A beautiful Hispanic woman walked toward her, breasts standing out proud and high and bare. Taylor smiled to think how the vice president of the Rotary Club and his wife would have reacted to the sight. Probably just as well that she'd booked them to Fort Lauderdale.

She spread her towel out on the lounger and untied her sarong. After Baltimore's frigid weather, the sun felt heavenly. Just for a little while, she'd give herself the luxury of lying out in it, before she yielded to reason and moved over into the shade.

Lying back on her couch, she sighed in pure bliss, listening to the soft rush of the waves, the breeze whispering through the palm fronds of the palapa. Reaching into her bag, she rummaged for the bottle of sun block. Even though with her brown eyes, she was the rare blonde who took to the sun readily, it paid to be careful in the tropics.

She spread sun block along her legs, idly watching a pair of topless women walking up the beach. What must it feel like to feel the sun on your bare breasts, on skin that hadn't felt the caress of the sun in years, if ever?

It was a surprisingly enticing notion, she thought as she smoothed the coconut-scented lotion along her arms. Intriguing.

Tempting.

A woman on a sun couch nearby chattered something in what sounded like Italian to her male companion and turned to lie on her back. He made a pretend grab for one of her breasts and she batted his hands away laughingly.

Taylor shook her head as she spread sun block on her neck and chest. The past was the past. She wasn't demoralized any more. She'd ignored her ex's rants and forced through the divorce. So what if marriage was just one more thing she hadn't finished? She'd been so focused on beating her family reputation as a quitter that she'd stayed in the marriage long after she'd realized it was toxic. Some things weren't meant to be finished. It was just as well that she'd gotten on with her life.

But had she? Taylor set the bottle in the sand. Had she really gotten with it? Until Bennett, she'd been quick to have a good time, quick to be outrageous. At 20, before she'd quit college to marry him, those qualities had drawn him at first, her sexiness, her wildness. That had all changed the day they'd made their vows. But since the split, she'd thrown herself into work, and later starting the business. That had taken all of her time and energy, leaving none for her private life.

No more, she thought in a sudden surge of recklessness. It was time to do something outrageous, after all, she was on vacation.

The Italian woman gave a magnificent roar of laughter, propping herself up on her elbows and giving her mane of hair a shake. Taylor lay down and closed her eyes. How Bennett would have hated the very idea of women sitting topless on a beach, though that wouldn't have stopped him from staring. And the very idea of Taylor doing anything so brazen, well, it would have given him a stroke.

A rush of daring whisked through her. Taylor's eyes opened and a slow smile spread across her face. Why shouldn't she? It wasn't as if anyone knew her here. She was thousands of miles from home. Going topless here was hardly outré—it was an accepted norm. And wouldn't it feel marvelous, she thought as the sun soaked into her bones. Wouldn't it be amazing to be so free?

Before she could back out, she sat up and reached back to unhook her bikini top, shrugging so that the shoulder straps fell down to dangle against her arms. She took a deep breath. And then it was off and her breasts were swaying free.

The skies didn't part with lightning to strike her. The nattily attired resort security guard didn't swoop down in agitation. Basically, no one noticed.

Except her. The breeze surprised her the most, the feel of air whispering lightly over skin unaccustomed to it. She felt wonderfully decadent and yet somehow comfortable. The sun was like a warm kiss, and she laughed at the feeling. Finally, long minutes later, she groped for the bottle of sun block. Skin that hadn't seen the sun since she'd been a toddler, if even then, needed all the protection it could get.

Leaning back on one elbow, she used the other hand to rub the lotion into her breast. She wouldn't feel bashful about touching herself, she told herself sternly. It was skin like any other on her body. And yet the feel of her lotion-slicked palm rubbing over her nipple made her system jolt.

Now there was a sad statement on her nonexistent love life, if just putting sun block on her breasts could turn her on. She was on vacation for heaven's sakes, maybe now was the perfect time for a fling?

And what a person could do with a lover in the tropics. Closing her eyes and settling back, Taylor relaxed, the light shining red orange through her lids. How would it be to have a man's hand stroking the sun block on her body slowly, teasingly, the delicious friction of skin against skin bringing her to arousal? Her imagination painted them naked on deserted beach, immersed in the feel of each other's bodies. Alone but for sun and sand, they reached for abandonment and beyond. His hand slid down over her breasts, across her belly, touching her the way she hadn't been touched in so long. The caress moved to her hips, up her thighs, slipping into the slick—

"Careful you don't get burned there. That skin's awfully pale," said a voice.

A male voice. A voice that was vaguely familiar, she thought with the first glimmer of uneasiness. The red haze of the sun on her eyelids had darkened, as though someone were casting a shadow over her.

She opened her eyes.

And saw Dev Carson grinning down at her.

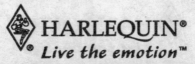

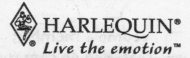

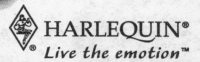

HARLEQUIN® *Temptation®*

*Legend has it that
the only thing that can bring down a Quinn
is a woman...*

Now we get to see for ourselves!

The youngest Quinn brothers have grown up.
They're smart, they're sexy...and they're about to be
brought to their knees by their one true love.

Don't miss the last three books in
Kate Hoffmann's dynamic miniseries...

The Mighty Quinns

Watch for:

THE MIGHTY QUINNS: LIAM
(July 2003)

THE MIGHTY QUINNS: BRIAN
(August 2003)

THE MIGHTY QUINNS: SEAN
(September 2003)

Available wherever Harlequin books are sold.

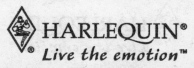

HARLEQUIN®
Live the emotion™

Visit us at www.eHarlequin.com

HTMQ

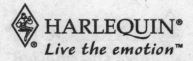